Om-kas-toe

Amazing Indian Children series:

Naya Nuki: Shoshoni Girl Who Ran
Om-kas-toe: Blackfeet Twin Captures an Elkdog
Soun Tetoken: Nez Perce Boy Tames a Stallion
Kunu: Winnebago Boy Escapes
Pathki Nana: Kootenai Girl Solves a Mystery
Moho Wat: Sheepeater Boy Attempts a Rescue
Amee-nah: Zuni Boy Runs the Race of His Life
Doe Sia: Bannock Girl and the Handcart Pioneers
Takini: Lakota Boy Alerts Sitting Bull

————————————

The Truth about Sacajawea, is an accurate paraphrase of the Lewis and Clark journal accounts of the remarkable Shoshoni teenager who spent twenty-one months with the Corps of Discovery. The United States Mint used this book when it developed the new Sacajawea Golden Dollar coin.

Om-kas-toe
Blackfeet Twin Captures an Elkdog

Kenneth
Thomasma

Ken Thomasma 2005

Jack
Brouwer
Illustrator

Grandview Publishing Company
Box 2863, Jackson, WY 83001

Copyright 1986, 1992 by Kenneth Thomasma

Tenth printing, June 2004

Library of Congress Cataloging-in-Publication Data

Thomasma, Kenneth.
    Om-kas-toe : Blackfeet twin captures an elkdog / Kenneth Thomasma ; Jack Brouwer, illustrator
      215 p.   cm. — (Amazing Indian children series)
      Summary: Life changes dramatically for the Blackfeet people in the early 1700s when a twin brother and sister discover a strange animal and succeed in bringing it back to the tribe.
      1. Siksika Indians — Juvenile fiction. [1. Siksika Indians — Fiction. 2. Indians of North America — Fiction. 3. Twins — Fiction. 4. Horses — Fiction.] I. Brouwer, Jack, ill. II. Title. III. Series: Amazing Indian children series.
PZ7.T3696Om   1986
[Fic]—dc20   89-14879

ISBN 1-880114-06-2 (Grandview Publishing Company)
ISBN 1-880114-05-4 (Grandview Publishing Company: pbk.)

Printed in the United States of America by Cushing-Malloy, Inc.

Grandview Publishing Company 1-800-525-7344

To

June and Bill Westbrook, Sr.,
and Susan and Bill Westbrook, Jr.,
for all their special help and friendship;

the boys and girls
of Kelly Elementary School for their questions
suggestions, and helping in naming each chapter;
and

Darnell Doore,
George and Molly Kicking Woman,
and Mary Ground,
my special Blackfeet friends,
for their valuable help.

Contents

Preface

Om-kas-toe (Om-käs-toe) is representative of Blackfeet Indian children who lived during "dog days" before the coming of the horse to their people.

Without historical fiction there would be no children's literature depicting life as it must have been for Indian boys and girls before the 1900s.

Writing about a period of history that dates back more than 280 years presented a challenge. The Indian people living on the northern plains just east of the Continental Divide had had no contact with white civilization. As a result there is no written history of their culture as it was in the very early 1700s.

The first mountain men to have contact with the Blackfeet people heard the elders talk about life during "dog days." Their accounts were sketchy at best.

Research for this book was done by reading several accounts scholars have written about "dog days." Each writer admits that much has to be left to speculation and educated guesses about life among the Blackfeet during this time.

Visits to actual sites of events in this story were valuable. The movement from summer hunting grounds on the prairies to the winter camps in the southern valleys is quite well documented by oral history and the archaeology of the area.

Mary Ground

Darnell Doore, George and Molly Kicking Woman, and Mary Ground, all members of the Blackfeet Tribe, were extremely kind and helpful. They gave me many details about their language and culture. The highlight of my research was my visit with

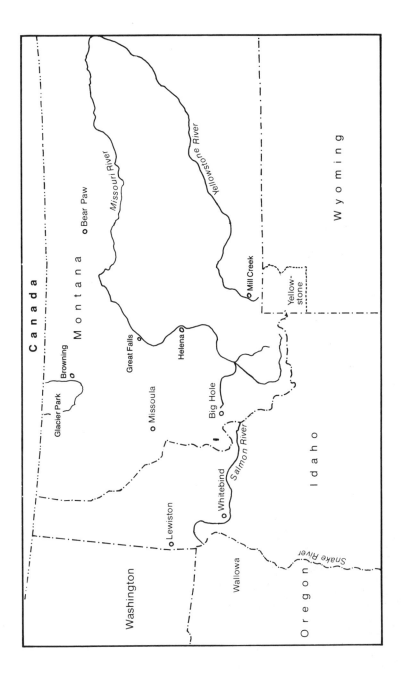

Mary Ground in the nursing home in Browning, Montana. Mary (aged 103) shared her vast experience and knowledge with me. Included in this visit was a beautiful prayer Mary offered for me in the Blackfeet language. Mary's daughter, Gertrude Heavy Runner, was kind enough to arrange the opportunity for me to meet her mother.

In writing about the Blackfeet people the word *Blackfoot* is never used. The accepted word is Blackfeet in all cases. Blackfoot is the name of a completely separate group of people today.

1

Twins and Wise Bird

A young Blackfeet Indian boy crouched quietly behind a fallen tree. He was watching a pack of wolves walk slowly up a hillside. The wolves were moving toward a small herd of mule deer. It was late winter and the wolves were very hungry. This pack would have to be clever to catch the speedy deer. A mule deer can leap long distances in a single jump. As soon as the deer saw the wolves, they would be gone, leaving the wolves far behind them.

This Indian boy knew he was watching a great hunt. Never before had he had a chance to see anything like he was about to witness. He was hidden in a perfect place where he could see the deer on one side of the small hill and the wolves stalking toward them from the opposite side of the same hill.

How would the wolves ever catch these deer? The deer were right out in the open. The wolves would have to show themselves before they got close to the deer. It didn't seem like the wolves had a chance.

This boy was about to learn a lesson about the wolf pack. He watched as the wolves came to a sudden stop. They came close together, almost as if they were having a meeting to decide what to do next.

In minutes, as if a signal had been given, the wolves started moving again. This time three of the eight wolves moved off to the left. Four others stalked to the right. Both groups stayed out of sight of the deer as they moved around each side of the hill.

The boy wondered why the wolves had split up. Why did one wolf stay in place?

The wolf that waited alone watched as the others moved far out on the sides of the sloping hill. At just the right time this lone wolf trotted to the top of the hill where the deer could see him easily. The six mule deer raised their heads quickly and looked at the wolf walking down the hill right at them. The lead doe watched this single wolf curiously for a few seconds. Then she turned to look around, sensing there could be greater danger nearby.

The big doe was right. She caught sight of the four wolves that had gone to the right. In an instant she bounded off with the other five deer close behind her.

Just as quickly as the deer had started their run, they stopped. Now they saw the other three wolves that had gone left. The frightened deer had no choice. They were forced to run straight ahead. The chase was on.

The boy saw how the clever wolves were forcing the deer to run right toward a large snowfield. On the dry ground the deer were leaving the wolves far behind. When the deer reached the deep snow, they lost their advantage. The snow had thawed during the day and then had frozen at night. This gave the snow a crust. The deer's hooves kept breaking through the crust. The deer were slowed down and the struggle to keep going tired them quickly. The hard winter had already made them weak.

As soon as the deer entered the snow, the wolves closed in on them. When the wolves got to the snow, they ran on top of the crusted surface without falling through. They were lighter than the deer and their webbed paws kept them from breaking the crust.

The boy watched the wolves pounce on the helpless deer. The kills were made quickly. The pack would enjoy a feast.

The boy had seen for himself how the wolves worked together to make the kill. Each wolf did its job. Their plan was perfect. One wolf alone could never have trapped the deer. The whole pack was needed, and the whole pack would enjoy the meat. The boy knew that his people always worked together also. They had to trap their game and make a kill or not have meat to eat. The small boy would never forget the hunt he had just watched.

Now he ran at top speed toward the camp. Hunters would have to hurry back to the snowfield to chase the wolves away and take the meat. Any chance to get fresh meat could not be missed. The boy's people never had much fresh meat in the winter months.

The boy who watched these wolves lived in the early 1700s, before the Blackfeet Indian people had any horses. All hunting was done on foot. It was difficult and dangerous. Winter made hunting even harder.

All Blackfeet boys were great runners. When they became men, their families would depend on their skills as hunters. Men were always ready for a hunt. Running was part of every hunt.

After the boy reached the camp with his news, the men followed him back to the scene of the kill. They had no trouble driving the wolves away. When they had a track broken through the snow, the men dragged the deer to the edge of the snowfield. The wolves had not eaten much of the meat, and they were angry about losing their kills. The pack prowled back and forth on the bare ridge above the snowfield. They watched as their food was taken from them.

This late winter morning had been an exciting one for this Blackfeet boy. He would soon begin his eighth summer. He was proud when the hunters said good things to him this day. He had made a great discovery for his people. They would all enjoy fresh meat because of his good luck. Before this day ended, an even greater thing would happen to the boy. This thing would change his life forever.

This eight-year-old was a twin. His name was Twin Boy. His sister was called Twin Girl. When the twins were born, it was seen as a bad thing. In those days Blackfeet people believed that the birth of twins was a great burden to the mother and to the whole band of people. With twins the mother would not be able to keep up with all her work. She would not be able to carry her share of the loads when the camp moved. She could not help with the buffalo hunts. Her husband could never help her with her work. The man needed to spend all his time hunting and protecting his people from enemy warriors.

When twins were born a boy and a girl, the people knew what the mother would have to do. She would keep the boy so he could grow strong, become a man, and learn to hunt and to fight the enemy. The girl would be left behind to die.

The mother of these twins was Tall Woman. Right away she begged the leaders of the village to let her keep both babies. She promised to do all her work as she always had. She told the men that she believed that the twins were a gift from the Above One. She believed the twins would bring good medicine to the band. Tall Woman pleaded and pleaded to be allowed to keep the tiny babies.

Tall Woman told the men that her ten-year-old daughter, Crooked Arm, would also work extra hard and help with the babies. The girl had been injured badly when a charging buffalo stepped on her. Her broken arm had healed with a bad bend just above her left wrist.

"Crooked Arm will not get a husband soon. She will help me with the babies. Oh! Please let us keep both of them. Don't make me leave the girl baby to die. Please, I give my heart and my life for my babies. All will be well. I beg you to let me keep both of my babies."

When the leaders met alone to decide what to do, most of the men said the girl baby must be left to die.

They argued that no woman could do all her work if she had two babies to care for. Also, the girl baby would take the mother's milk that the boy would need to grow strong. A weak boy would never grow up to be a strong hunter.

Only one man had not spoken yet. He had listened to all the arguments before he rose from his seat to speak. He was the oldest man in the band. His name was Old Man. Everyone listened carefully as he spoke.

"Tall Woman has been a good woman all her life. She does her work well. She carries heavy loads and does not complain. She packs her dogs quickly and well. She even helps others when they have need. Tall Woman causes her husband to be proud. I have not seen a better woman in all the years of my long life. Let her keep both babies. Soon we will see if she is right when she says she can do all her work as before and still care for the two tiny ones. Our answer will come soon. Brothers, we can let the days ahead give us our wisdom."

Old Man's words were so wise that no one could speak against them. The leaders agreed. They would wait to see if Tall Woman could really do all her work and not become a burden to her husband, Otterman, or the band. They would wait to see if good or evil would come from their decision.

Tall Woman was the happiest mother on earth. She had her chance. Nothing would stop her from proving she could take care of both babies and still do all her work.

No one ever worked harder than Tall Woman and Crooked Arm. There wasn't a single person who could find fault with their work. No bad thing happened to the band after the twins were both allowed to live. In fact many good things happened. Hunting was never better. Dogs pulled their travois as before. No lives were lost nor were there any serious injuries to any of the people. Life went on as it always had. Soon the leaders stopped talking about the twin children.

Twin Boy helped carry the deer meat back to the camp. He enjoyed his share of the fresh meat. He was also happy to listen to the men talk about his great discovery.

That afternoon Twin Boy left the camp with his father, Otterman. They set out to gather serviceberry stems to use for making arrows. They would also be on the look-out for deer, elk, moose, and other animals to hunt.

Twin Boy was proud to go with his father. Otterman did not speak much. When he did say something, Twin Boy listened carefully to every word. Otterman taught his son many things. The boy learned most by watching, listening, and remembering. He copied everything his father did. When Twin Boy spoke he even sounded like Otterman.

The father and son ran at a steady pace toward a meadow near the river. The morning had been cold but the day was warming fast. The wind started blowing. Dark clouds rolled over the ridges in the south and the west. A storm was coming to the whole valley.

Otterman signaled to Twin Boy to work quickly. He wanted to be back to the camp before the storm hit. They worked fast, picking out the best stems they could find. The wood needed to be just the right size and as straight as possible.

Quickly the clouds moved over the entire valley. The wind became much stronger. Next came sleet.

"Take your wood. We return to camp. Run!"

Otterman's words sent Twin Boy into motion. With his serviceberry stems held in his right hand, the boy ran stride for stride with his father across the valley toward the camp. Now the wind blew fiercely. The sleet made the ground slippery.

Twin Boy lost his footing and fell. He put his hands down to break his fall. His arrow shafts scattered over the ground.

Otterman did not see his son fall and he ran on to the village. Twin Boy got to his feet quickly and began picking up his bundle of wood. Suddenly he stopped and stood very still. He saw something fluttering on the ground near a tree.

Twin Boy put his arrow shafts down and ran over for a closer look. There on the ground lay a young raven that had been hurt when its nest came down in the wind. One wing was out of place. The little raven could not hold this wing close to its body. The frightened bird flapped its good wing wildly as the boy came closer. It opened its beak and squawked at Twin Boy, trying to scare him away.

Twin Boy moved quickly. He dropped to his knees and carefully but swiftly picked up the frightened bird. The raven struggled to escape. The boy held it firmly but gently. Twin Boy was especially careful not to hurt the injured wing. He held the raven close to his body and walked as fast as he could to the camp.

Twin Boy was so excited that he could not remember much of his walk back to camp. He had forgotten all about his arrow shafts.

The boy hurried to his lodge to show the raven to his mother and his sisters. He asked Twin Girl to hold the bird while he quickly formed a makeshift cage. Tall Woman let him use a large woven basket. Twin Boy made a cover for the basket out of sticks tied together.

Twin Girl lowered the little raven to the bottom of the basket. The young bird had already calmed down a lot. It seemed to be losing some of its fear.

Twin Boy cut some deer meat into small pieces for the raven and gave it some water. But the bird showed no interest in food or water.

In the days ahead Twin Boy spent a lot of time with the young raven. He made him his own cage by weaving

many willow branches together. In a few days the raven ate for the first time. Each day the injured wing seemed a little better. Soon it seemed to be all healed.

The raven was also becoming tame. It would eat from Twin Boy's hand. The boy let the raven out of its cage to feed for the first time. The bird made no effort to escape and returned to its cage willingly. Soon Twin Boy had the bird out for long periods of time.

Everyone in this band of 130 Blackfeet Indians knew the legends of the raven they called Big Crow. The coming of this raven could do nothing but bring good luck to its owner and the people of his band. Ravens were good medicine in the stories heard around Blackfeet fires.

In the next year the boy and his raven were always seen together. Often the raven would perch on the boy's shoulder and eat from his hand. The raven grew fast and learned many tricks. Twin Boy played the raven's favorite game every day. The raven loved to retrieve small sticks or pieces of hide thrown by the boy.

Twin Boy named the raven Wise Bird, because it even seemed to understand many of the words the boy spoke, and it learned new tricks quickly.

Twin Girl also spent much of her spare time playing with Wise Bird. The raven's favorite landing place was the top of Twin Girl's head. He would hang on to her hair and pick away at the tiny shells or bones that Twin Girl always had tied in her hair. The young girl with the raven sitting on her head was a sight the Blackfeet people could never get used to. They were amazed at the coming of the raven to the twin children. Their amazement would grow beyond belief in the years ahead.

2

A Desperate Search

A whole year had passed since Twin Boy had found Wise Bird. Now another winter was ending. Twin Boy had waited what seemed like an extra-long time to hear some special words. The exciting words were spoken by Old Man, the beloved leader of the band of Blackfeet Indians.

"Winter is ending. Tomorrow we move our camp. Again we follow the buffalo to his summer home on the great open lands. Everyone must be ready. All must work hard to make our journey a good one."

Twin Boy left the cooking fire that night and went straight to his tepee and his bed. Wise Bird found his perch, and they slept.

The next morning was bitter cold, but winter really was giving way to spring. There was excitement throughout the camp. Hungry dogs were staked out. They pulled at their hide tethers and barked as loudly as they could. Even the dogs knew this was the big day, the day to move.

Twin Boy hurried to give the dogs a meal of dried meat. He knew the camp would soon be packed. The dogs would be harnessed with hide straps under their stomachs and across their chests. Next two travois poles would be slipped into hide loops above the dogs' shoulders and the loops would be tied tightly. In the early 1700s the Blackfeet people had only dogs to carry their loads. They did not have a single horse or even know what one looked like.

Dogs were not able to carry very heavy loads on their travois. Each family could carry just enough to use to survive and little extra. What the dogs could not carry had to be carried on the backs of women and children.

Men carried only weapons. Each man had to be ready at a moment's notice to run at top speed if buffalo or other game animals were seen. The men also had to be ready to defend their people from their enemies. The men needed to have their arms and legs free to go into action to help their families survive each day.

Soon everyone was busy making packs of all their belongings. Large packs were tied to the dogs' travois. Smaller packs were carried by women and children. Mothers with small babies wrapped their tiny ones in soft hides. The child was tied into a cradleboard. The cradleboard was then tied on top of the pack on the travois. This made it possible for the woman to carry a heavy pack on her back. At the same time the mother could hold the tether that held the dog.

Dogs barked. Women shouted orders to the children. The air was filled with noise and excitement. Twin Boy held the ropes of two dogs, trying to keep them away from other dogs. The dogs were half wild. They loved a good fight. They had to be watched every second. Most of them could not be trusted at all.

Twin Boy looked up to see Wise Bird flying in a great circle above the noisy camp. Soon he would land in a dead cottonwood tree to watch and wait.

As Twin Boy looked up, he didn't see a dog behind him getting very close to a dog he was holding. The boy looked back just in time to pull his dog away. He shouted at Twin Girl.

"Pull Whiteface back. He wants a fight!"

Twin Girl gripped the braided leather and gave it a jerk.

"Back, Whiteface! Back!" she yelled.

The dog felt the hard pull on the tether and sat back, barking and growling. His upper lip was raised, showing his yellowing teeth.

When all was ready, Runs-Like-Antelope, the band's best hunter and warrior, led a group of men away from the camp. These were the strongest and fastest warriors. They would go ahead of the people to look for game to hunt and to scout for danger from enemy warriors. Other men would go out on each side of the line of dogs to do the same thing. A few older warriors were on guard behind the people. The twins' father led the warriors on the right of the moving line of people and dogs.

As the first dogs started moving, every dog jumped to its feet and began tugging on its tether. The barking was louder than ever. Women and children had all they could do to hold the eager dogs back. This first day was always the hardest.

Twin Boy took one last look at the winter campsite. It was built in a clearing surrounded by spruce trees that grew close to a steep mountainside. The site had been picked because there was good water nearby, plenty of firewood, and very little wind. Moose, elk, deer, and buffalo could be hunted in the surrounding valleys. The site was near present-day Ennis, Montana, and the Madison River.

It was a good winter camp, but Twin Boy was happy to leave. Summer always meant more to eat and a chance to see good friends from other bands. The Blackfeet people gathered every summer in large groups to help each other hunt the buffalo on the great open lands.

As the line of dogs, women, children, and old people moved through the valley, the dogs calmed down. They pulled their loads forward steadily and quietly. Women and children kept them apart so no two dogs could get at each other.

Several stops were made to tighten loads or to pick up items that fell from the travois. Everyone holding a dog's lead also had to be ready to hang on to their dogs in case one of them should see a rabbit, an antelope, or some other animal. With one quick lunge, a dog could pull free and be gone after an animal, leaving the rest far behind.

Twin Boy and Twin Girl carried loads on their backs, and each held a dog in the line as the people moved slowly along the valley floor. A faint trail used by people and animals was followed. Large patches of snow covered the hillsides here and there. The high mountains were still completely covered with a thick blanket of snow.

As the day went on people and dogs began to get tired. This first day of travel after a long winter would be short. Camp would be made early. The next day the people would go a little farther. In a few days the band would be traveling up to eight miles a day.

In midafternoon, just before the band found a campsite, the lead dog came over a gentle slope and saw three antelope in the meadow below. The big dog lurched forward, pulling his lead from the woman's hand before she could brace herself. The dog and his travois were gone in an instant. The woman screamed. Everyone pulled their dogs to a halt.

The terrified woman threw off her backpack and ran at top speed through the sagebrush after the fleeing dog. As she ran she continued to scream. The people all knew why she was frantic. The dog that got away from this woman carried her one-year-old baby on his travois. She hoped her screams would bring the warriors. They could stop the dog and save her baby.

The three antelope bounded away with the charging dog behind them. The ground was a series of rolling hills. Soon the dog and the antelope left the poor woman far behind.

The child carried on the dog's travois was safely wrapped in a cradleboard. The cradleboard was tied tightly to the travois, but at the speed the dog was traveling the travois bounced wildly. Soon the whole thing began to break apart, and piece by piece it broke away. It was scattered over a great distance.

The cradleboard landed in the sagebrush. It hit a large bush, saving the baby from serious injury. The cradleboard came to rest beneath the huge brush. The child was lying face up, completely out of sight. The baby cried for a short time and then fell asleep.

When the woman lost sight of the dog, she dashed back to the waiting line of people. She cried out loudly, asking everyone to help her find her baby. The people had already tied their dogs and put down their packs, and were ready to begin the search. Two boys were sent running to find the warriors so they could help.

The dog's tracks were hard to follow through the sagebrush. People spread out and walked over the ground where they thought the child might be. Twin Girl was the first to discover part of the broken travois. She shouted to the other searchers to come. The child's mother found a second travois pole a quarter of a mile farther north. Two warriors found part of the load.

The people looked carefully all around the places where these items were found. Surely the child must be close by. Twin Boy had heard stories of children who were never found after one of these terrible accidents.

The searchers did not realize that this baby had been thrown off the travois very soon after the dog began the chase. The pieces of the travois actually caused the searchers to look in the wrong place.

As the search went on without success, the frantic mother pleaded with the leaders not to give up. They promised to make camp nearby so the search could go on. They planned to search until dark and then stay up all night to keep any wild animals away.

Gray Feather was the band's beaver medicine man. The people believed he had special powers which could heal the sick, bring good luck to hunters, and work many other miracles. The beaver was a sacred animal of the Blackfeet in those days. Gray Feather went off by himself to ask the powers of the beaver to help the people find the baby.

The afternoon was passing quickly. If the baby spent the night in the open, he could die from the cold or a wild animal might find him. He must be found before dark.

Twin Boy was very tired, but when he saw the child's mother searching frantically for her baby, he knew he had to keep looking. The boy had not seen Wise Bird for some time. He wondered where the raven was. Just then the graceful bird swooped from the sky and landed on Twin Boy's shoulder.

"Wise Bird, have you come to help find the baby?"

Twin Boy had asked the question without even thinking. Suddenly he looked straight into the eyes of the big bird.

"That's it! Wise Bird, you can find the baby!"

The raven cocked his head from side to side as if he were trying to understand the boy.

"Stay!" shouted Twin Boy as he turned and began climbing an open ridge to get above the searchers. Wise Bird clung to the boy's right wrist as the boy rushed up the ridge.

At the top Twin Boy stood and looked at the searchers scattered over the valley floor. He looked at Wise Bird. With his left arm he made a large sweeping motion across his body, pointing his finger at the searchers below.

"Baby! Find the baby! Wise Bird, find the baby!"

Again the raven cocked his head from side to side as he watched and listened. Twin Boy often played games with Wise Bird. The raven loved to find objects the boy had thrown into the sagebrush. Wise Bird would fetch the object every time.

Today ravens are known to be one of the smartest of all birds. They have even been trained to use simple tools to get food. They love to play games.

Twin Boy did not realize that what was about to happen would be one of the greatest miracles his people would ever witness. Just as the boy did when he played with Wise Bird for fun, he used the word *find* over and over.

"Find the baby! Find the baby! Wise Bird, find!"

Twin Boy even cried like a baby to help Wise Bird understand. With a sweep of the arm the raven was sitting on the boy shouted, "Go! Find the baby! Wise Bird, find! Go! Find!"

Wise Bird took off, spread his great wings, and soared down the hillside. He made two huge circles over the searchers. It's working, the boy thought as his eyes followed the raven's flight. Then at the end of the second circle Wise Bird suddenly turned and flew away.

Where is he going? Has Wise Bird given up already? Is he off hunting for food? Doesn't he understand? Twin Boy felt badly as he watched the raven leave. Wise Bird was headed back toward the line of waiting dogs and started flying in circles not far from the dogs.

Twin Boy thought to himself that Wise Bird might still be trying. Surely he would fail. The child could not have fallen way back there. That was a place the dog had passed soon after the chase had begun.

Twin Boy was ready to start down the hill to rejoin the searchers when he saw Wise Bird quickly tuck his wings and drop on a sharp angle toward the ground below. Just before reaching the ground, the raven spread its shiny black wings and made a soft landing on a tall sagebrush bush.

Wise Bird sat there flapping his wings and squawking as loudly as he could. Twin Boy stopped in his tracks. He couldn't take his eyes off the raven. He knew the bird's call. It was the same call he had heard many times when

Wise Bird had found an object the boy had thrown into the bushes.

He's found something. It couldn't be the baby. Not that far back. As Twin Boy thought about it, he saw Twin Girl running at full speed toward the raven. Twin Girl had watched Wise Bird's flight. When he landed, she said to herself, That's it! We have all looked in the wrong place! The child fell off the travois way back there. Wise Bird has found the baby!

Mysteriously these same thoughts came to Twin Boy. He, too, was running toward the raven as fast as he could go down the sage-covered ridge.

Twin Girl got to Wise Bird first. She dropped to her knees. Twin Boy came running up at the very moment that Twin Girl saw the end of a cradleboard sticking out from under the sagebrush bush. She grabbed the cradleboard and pulled it into the open. There she saw the most beautiful sight she had ever seen. It was the lost baby smiling happily.

Twin Boy didn't even wait to catch a breath. He turned in great excitement and, running faster than he ever had before, cleared one sagebrush after another.

"The baby has been found! The baby has been found!" shouted the high-stepping boy.

Quickly the news spread. The people watched as the mother ran to meet Twin Girl who was hurrying toward her with the precious bundle. The mother took her baby from Twin Girl. Tears of joy streamed down the mother's face as she held her baby to her breast.

Everyone shared the mother's joy. The baby was unhurt. Soon the whole story was told. The boy and his raven had found the child. It was a miracle! Every detail of the story was told again and again. Twin Boy never tired of answering questions and telling his story.

At the campfire that night, Old Man reminded the people about the birth of the twins. He talked about Tall Woman's great love. Truly the Above One had rewarded the goodness and hard work of this mother.

That night Twin Boy was called to stand before the people at the campfire. A name-giving ceremony began. Several leaders stood to speak. One after another they spoke of the boy's special gift of being able to speak to Wise Bird. They said the spirits had picked Twin Boy to be the one to receive the special gift of this great bird.

Each man retold the story of the lost baby, the search, the tears of the mother, and the miracle of the raven. This was the greatest miracle the people had ever experienced.

At the end of his speech each leader said, "My son, from this day on you have a new name. Take the name Om-kas-toe, meaning raven. By this name all will remember the great thing you have done this day."

Then each man took a turn standing in front of the boy. Each one put his hand out to rest on the boy's shoulder and said, "May your life be long, Om-kas-toe."

After the ceremony and all the greetings the boy received, he stood silently. Om-kas-toe, Om-kas-toe, he said over and over to himself. It would take many days to get used to this new name, but this Blackfeet boy would never forget this day.

3

A Dangerous Hunt

The days of travel north were long and full of work for everyone. The best days were those when the hunters came back with deer, elk, or moose meat. Very few buffalo were seen in the valleys.

When Om's people reached the open lands far to the north, they would camp near other bands of Blackfeet Indian people. All summer the men would roam the rolling grasslands in search of buffalo. They were dangerous to hunt. It took many hunters to surround the herds on foot and make the kills. Sometimes the huge beasts could be stampeded over cliffs. At other times special corrals were built to drive buffalo into so the men could get to them.

When a corral was built, it was designed carefully so it could hold the powerful buffalo. The largest animals weighed more than twelve hundred pounds. If the corral was not strong enough, the beasts could break out quickly and escape.

After the corral fence was built, logs were sharpened at one end and stuck through the fence pointing right at chest level on the buffalo. If an animal charged the fence, it would be speared on one of these pointed logs. The other end of the pointed log was braced in the ground, so it could stop even the biggest of the beasts.

To get the buffalo into the corral the Indians made a large V-shaped runway bordered by two walls of bushes, rocks, and dead trees. The walls were laid out so the opening to the V was very wide, often more than three hundred yards. From that opening the walls led up a gentle slope. Along this slope the runway narrowed quite sharply. At the top of the slope the walls were very close together and led straight downhill into the corral.

Om and every member of the band had a job to do during the hunt. As soon as a herd of buffalo was found close to the corral, a hunter ran to the village to tell all the people to come quickly. They always ran toward the corral in a direction from which the wind would not carry their scent to the buffalo. The huge animals have poor eyesight but a good sense of smell.

The women and children and old people hid behind the V-shaped walls. When the hunters ran behind the buffalo and drove them between the walls, the people all jumped up, shouting and waving pieces of hide. This was done to keep the beasts away from the walls so they would not break through and escape. Once the men had the animals in the corral, they could run in and spear them. This was dangerous, and the men had to be fast on their feet to stay away from the sharp horns and huge hooves of the animals. Often a warrior was gored or kicked during this wild battle in the corral.

An even more exciting and dangerous hunt took place when a small band worked alone on a buffalo surround. When buffalo were sighted, women, children, and old people came to a well-chosen place with their travois poles. Just out of sight of the buffalo a C-shaped corral was made. The people put the travois poles on end into the ground to form the fence. Ropes were tied from pole to pole to hold them in place.

When the fence was ready, two fast runners came up behind the buffalo. These brave men chased the animals toward the corral. The rest of the hunters waited on both sides of the way to the quickly-made corral. The runners tried to chase only a few buffalo into this flimsy corral.

As the buffalo neared the people and their fence, the warriors on the sides stood and shouted and waved their spears. When the charging animals entered the cor-ral, the children and people behind the fence shouted, waved hides, and ran back and forth to keep the beasts inside the corral and away from the travois-pole fence. The hunters rushed in to kill the confused animals. This kind of a buffalo surround was the most dangerous of all. Only a few animals could be killed before the rest made their escape.

It was a cool, damp day as Om walked beside his dog's travois. The people were in their twentieth day on the trail north. They were about fifty miles north of the present-day city of Helena, Montana. They were coming into the open lands and good buffalo-hunting grounds.

Everything was going along as usual when Om heard the call that sent him and all the people into action. Buffalo were sighted. Tie the dogs. Unload the travois. Take poles, ropes, and dogs, and follow Redhawk. He will lead you to the best place to build the corral.

Very few words were spoken. Everyone knew what to do. The oldest people stayed with the tiny children and many of the dogs. Some of the hunters helped the women and older children erect the fence. When all was ready, Om watched the hunters take up their weapons and run to their places. He longed for the day when he too could take his spear and bow and arrows and be a real hunter. He even dreamed of being picked to run behind the huge beasts and chase them into the trap. Then he would run behind them into the corral and with a powerful thrust drive his spear into a mighty buffalo.

Right now Om, Twin Girl, and the rest of the women and children could only wait quietly and hope the hunt would be successful. The wait always seemed much longer than it really was.

Om's eyes were fastened on a gentle slope right in front of the corral fence he was crouched behind. Hunters were hiding in the grass on both sides of the slope. They were waiting for the two runners to drive the buffalo between them and into the corral.

It was so quiet. Had the runners failed to get the animals moving in the right direction? Did we do all this work for nothing? Will this day end with a feast or will we once again eat dried meat and roots at our evening meal? Om's mind wandered as he waited tensely, hoping for some action. The boy looked at the dog next to him. It was quietly chewing a piece of dried meat. The dog's barking would help keep the buffalo back from the fence if the men ever got any into the corral. Om remembered many times before when all the work was done and no buffalo were ever chased into the trap. He hoped this would not happen this time.

The first sounds Om heard were the distant shouts of the two runners. Then came the sound of hoofbeats on the ground. In seconds the first buffalo topped the gentle slope. Its shaggy head bobbed just inches from the ground. Its massive shoulders and back rose high above the horns on its head.

When five more stampeding animals came into view, the hunters on each side stood up straight, shouting and waving their weapons high above their heads. Down the slope came the frightened beasts. Just as they entered the corral, all the women and children jumped up and began shouting and waving pieces of hide. This caused the terrified buffalo to turn inches before they hit the corral fence. They milled around in great confusion, trying to decide where to run next.

Om could see the small eyes in the great shaggy heads as the panic-stricken animals milled around just inches away from him. The hunters closed in, cutting off any retreat. They started the kill. In minutes three of the six buffalo lay fatally wounded.

Om watched all this as he shouted loudly and waved a large elk hide. Then he saw a sight he would remember the rest of his life. The largest bull buffalo, its giant head only inches from the ground, came charging straight at

him. Om kept waving and shouting even as he looked into the eyes of the charging beast.

The last thing Om remembered doing was jumping quickly to his right to get out of the way of certain death. What happened next seemed like a bad dream. The big bull hit the fence with all its weight and power, breaking through and plowing right over the top of Om. The boy was knocked backward. He hit the ground and bounced under the belly of the great beast like a rag doll. The buffalo's sharp horns barely missed goring the boy to death. Its hooves landed inches from his body.

After the buffalo escaped, the boy lay still and limp on the ground. It was hours later when Om first opened his eyes. He didn't know how he had gotten to this bed. Camp had been set up close to the scene of the hunt. Tall Woman, Crooked Arm, and Twin Girl sat nearby. Om heard their voices, but could not hear what they were saying.

The boy hurt all over, especially his head. His arms and legs were sore, and his back ached. Om's eyes seemed out of focus. Everything looked blurry. His mind was fuzzy as he tried to remember what had happened.

Crooked Arm glanced at Om. She saw him move his arm and open his eyes.

"Mother, he's waking up!" cried Crooked Arm.

Tall Woman moved quickly to Om's side. Looking into his blinking eyes, she asked, "Can you hear me, my son?"

"Yes, Mother, I hear you," the boy answered softly.

"The Above One was with you today. The death spirit could not claim you. You were protected. Death passed close to you, my son."

"What happened, Mother?" whispered Om.

"The buffalo broke through the corral. He knocked you backward and passed right over you. One of his great hooves struck the dog that stood at your side. The dog was killed. You still live. Your mother gives thanks to the spirit that saved you from death this day."

After speaking, Om's mother gave the boy a sip of water. She wiped his face with a damp piece of soft hide. She would care for her son until he recovered. The band decided to stay in this camp for several days. Three large buffalo had been killed. Hundreds of pounds of meat needed drying. Hides needed to be scraped. The animals' horns were cut off and cleaned out. Small bones were saved to be used as needles. Tendons which hold the animals' muscles to their bones were stripped off to be used in sewing hides together and in making clothes. The people wasted no usable parts of the animals.

Om had suffered a concussion and had many bruises over his body. He had lots of pain and dizziness. In those days there were no modern medicines, doctors, or hospitals. Herbs and animal parts were used to help with healing, but many people died from injuries, infections, and disease.

The extra days in this camp were exactly what Om needed. The rest and care given him by his mother would help him recover from his concussion and bruises. Wise Bird kept the boy company, sitting by his side for hours each day. In two days Om was on his feet and moving around a little. Even though he hurt all over, it felt good to be back on his feet again. His strength was returning quickly. He would be ready to take his place in the long line of dogs and people moving north again. He was happy to be alive.

Om looked forward to the day his people would arrive at their favorite summer camp. It was a beautiful camp on a creek we call Two Medicine Creek today. Om loved this place. The mountains to the west were called the backbone of the earth by his people. They believed that many spirits dwelled in the high peaks of the spectacular mountains. These beautiful peaks are now part of Glacier National Park. Not only was there great beauty all around, but also hunting was excellent. There were buffalo, but also many deer, elk, moose, and other game animals. The people loved the thin soft hides of the deer and antelope. Each hide had special uses. Om loved summer and the excitement it brought him every year.

4

The Enemy and Elkdog

It was a good summer. Om saw all his friends from other bands. Many buffalo were killed. There was plenty of fresh meat and much work to do. Hides were scraped and tanned. Tools were made from bones of animals, from stones, and from sticks. Stones were used for points on arrows and spears. Large stones were found for tomahawk heads. Much time was spent finding the right stones. New travois poles were always needed. Women cut hides and sewed new clothes for winter. Extra moccasins were cut and sewn.

Like everyone, Om was busy all summer. There wasn't much time to play. Evening fires with stories and simple dances were a favorite time for everyone. Fresh meat every day was a real treat. Sometimes Om even got some buffalo tongue. It was his favorite. Wise Bird was always there for his share of the delicious meat. Om found time to play with the raven each day.

Summer days always passed quickly and soon the band was packed and moving south for another winter. Again the dogs pulled the loaded travois. Women and older children shouldered heavy loads. Warriors traveled light, ready to hunt or to fight off enemy warriors.

Om felt stronger than ever. During the summer, he became a better runner. He could run farther and faster than ever before. His arms could lift heavier loads. He was growing fast. Like his mother, Tall Woman, he was going to be taller than most men. Always he had been bigger than most boys his age. Soon he would be grown up enough to become a hunter and a warrior. No longer would he have to stay with the line of dogs while the men ran free with their weapons.

The move south was slow and easy, seven or eight miles a day. Many times several nights were spent at the same camp. Om was kept extra busy training a new dog. Teaching a half-wild dog to pull a travois was not easy. This dog was different, though. He was smart and seldom caused any trouble. He was a big dog and looked much like a wolf. Twin Girl had raised him since he was a puppy. He was one of six puppies born during a summer storm the year before. She named him Thunder.

Thunder was the easiest dog Om had ever had to train. The dog was so gentle he even let Wise Bird sit on his back. The raven could be fed a piece of meat with Thunder standing close by. The big dog never went after Wise Bird's food. Any other dog would kill the raven for a bite of meat. Thunder was fast becoming a favorite dog in the village.

In the middle of October the Blackfeet people moved through a wide valley southwest of present-day Great Falls, Montana. They traveled alongside a small river. This stream is called the Dearborn River today. It flows southeast into the Big Water, which we now call the Missouri River.

The day was clear and cool. It was just past the middle of the day. Om thought he heard a distant voice. Then he heard shouts. Over a ridge a runner came at top speed. Om heard his shouted warning.

"The enemy is near! Everyone move to a safe place! Hide the dogs! Women and children stay hidden with them!"

The Snake warriors were first spotted by Otterman, Om's father. Otterman watched as the enemy came straight toward him. If they weren't stopped, they would walk right into the Blackfeet people.

The enemy had not seen Otterman or any of the Blackfeet. Their scouts hadn't done a very good job. Otterman was well hidden behind an uprooted tree.

Otterman had to act fast. He quickly signaled the other warriors near him. They sent runners to warn the people and to get the rest of the Blackfeet warriors. Silently the warriors took their places in a long line behind the top of the long ridge.

The enemy had just come over a ridge in the distance. They were going to cross the valley floor and come right to the ridge where the Blackfeet warriors were hidden.

Meanwhile Om led his loaded dog away from the river with his people. They hurried into the trees that covered the hillside. Dogs were tied far from each other. They were given dried meat to chew to keep them quiet. Any sound could be heard by the enemy. Staying quiet and hidden was absolutely necessary.

Om knew his father and all the warriors would fight bravely. If they had to, they would die fighting for their families.

The Blackfeet warriors watched and waited as the enemy came closer. They counted twenty-six Snake warriors crossing the valley floor, but more might be coming. The Blackfeet sent scouts out to circle the whole valley in search of more enemy braves. The scouts were careful to stay out of sight and return as soon as they did their dangerous work.

Om was sitting close to Thunder. Wise Bird, quietly eating his piece of meat, was perched in a dead cottonwood tree. Om listened to every sound. Waiting was hard. The boy would give anything to be able to be out there doing something to help. Someday he, too, would stand and fight for this people. How he wished he could leave these trees now and stand beside his father and fight.

As these thoughts went through the boy's mind, he was startled by the touch of a hand on his shoulder. Om turned and looked up. There above him he saw the face of White Wolf, a warrior. The man took the surprised boy by the arm and pulled him to his feet.

"Om, come. We will scout the way ahead for our people. You will be runner. You will carry my message to our warriors. Your legs are strong. Come!"

Even before Om had time to get excited, he was running behind White Wolf through the trees. They ran past dogs, women, and children. Om saw Twin Girl holding Whiteface's tether tightly. The big dog was asleep. Twin Girl smiled at her brother. She knew Om was getting the chance he wanted so badly. Soon Om-kas-toe would be a real warrior.

The boy's eyes searched the hills as he and White Wolf ran hard. It is not easy to run over strange ground and look around at the same time. It is easy to trip and fall. Good balance was important to the speedy runners.

The ridge that White Wolf was following led southeast along the river valley. This warrior did not run as fast as he did as a young man, but he could still go many miles at a steady pace without stopping. Om knew his job was to follow and be ready to do whatever White Wolf asked him to do.

Far behind these two runners, the hidden Blackfeet warriors saw their great warrior, Runs-Like-Antelope, give the signal to stand and fight. All together the twenty-six Blackfeet men stood. Side by side they walked to the top of the ridge that had hidden them from their enemy.

The Snake warriors saw the Blackfeet right away. They stopped, moved back a little, spread out, and formed their own line.

Both sides knew they did not have enough men to charge the enemy. If one side far outnumbered the other, they would attack immediately. When the sides were nearly equal, each would stand and fight from a safe distance. Neither side would try to win. They were satisfied to shoot a few arrows and hold their ground. At darkness both sides would retreat and go their separate ways. This is what would happen on this day.

White Wolf finally stopped running. He had come to a high point on the long ridge. A large rock made a good lookout platform. White Wolf climbed gracefully to the top of this flat rock and crouched close to its edge.

After looking in every direction, White Wolf said, "We will lead our people this way. I see no enemy as far as my eyes can look."

Below Om listened and watched. He waited for White Wolf to speak again. He knew his job. To be silent, listen, and do all that White Wolf commanded was Om's duty.

The man did not move after he spoke. The boy saw White Wolf tense. The man was strangely still and silent. Then White Wolf rose up on one knee. He stared at one spot in the distance for a long time.

"Om! Come!"

As White Wolf spoke, he reached down, took the boy's arm, and pulled him up on the rock.

"Om-kas-toe! Look! What do you see? Do my eyes lie to me?"

It took Om a few seconds to see what White Wolf was talking about with such excitement. Then far off to the left Om saw what White Wolf saw. There in the distance were three enemy warriors moving north. They weren't walking. They were sitting on the backs of animals. The animals carried them over the ground while the men just sat on their backs. What kind of an animal could it be? Om strained his eyes to see every detail. The animals looked like elk, but they carried the men like dogs carry loads.

White Wolf and Om both stared at this strange scene. They saw the warriors stop their animals and slide to the ground. Each warrior held his animal by a rope, much as a dog is held.

White Wolf finally spoke. "The warriors ride the elk, but these elk have long tails like the dog. These elk act like dogs. They do not run from the men. What animal can this be?"

Om listened to White Wolf's words. The boy could not understand what his eyes were telling him. He was sure this was some great magic. It seemed like a dream.

The man and boy watched as one warrior held the ropes of all three animals while the other two went to the stream for a drink. The two drank, filled a hide bag, and returned to their animals. All three men jumped to the backs of their animals and rode from sight.

White Wolf and Om stayed on the rock. Neither said a word. Each was trying to understand what he had just seen with his own eyes.

"Elkdogs. Elkdogs," said White Wolf.

Om listened to this strange name. Elkdog sounded as unusual as this animal looked.

In an instant White Wolf jumped from the rock, motioned to Om to follow, and began running back to the waiting people. The sun was setting. Darkness would come soon. The people must move now to a safe camp for the night.

White Wolf left Om with the line of dogs. The warrior ran on to give his report to Runs-Like-Antelope.

Soon the people had the dogs moving. Staying in the trees, they traveled away from the battle lines. At dark camp was made in the pine trees at the base of a steep cliff. No fires were started. Guards were posted all night to watch and listen for the enemy.

News of the strange animal, elkdog, spread through the camp. It was hard to believe White Wolf's story. How could a man ride on an elk? White Wolf was a trusted scout and warrior. All his life he never lied to his people. He would tell only the truth. And the boy, Om, he saw them, too. What strange medicine did the enemy have?

The first time the Blackfeet people saw the horse they called it elkdog. In the Blackfeet language today the horse is still called elkdog.

The coming of the elkdog would soon change how every Blackfeet would live. That night Om dreamed he was sitting on an elkdog riding over the land. It was the strangest and most exciting dream he ever had. The boy wondered if he would ever see elkdogs again. His mind would be filled with thoughts about elkdogs every day from that time on. He was sure he would not just see elkdogs again but that someday he would sit upon one and ride it across the same trails he traveled each year.

5

Wise Bird's Secret

Om's people made it to their winter camp safely. They did not see their enemies again. Neither did they see any more elkdogs. Many nights that winter White Wolf was asked to tell his story about the day he saw the three warriors with their elkdogs. He told every single detail of what he saw from his rock. Om was asked to tell his part each time White Wolf finished. The boy enjoyed telling the story as much as the people loved hearing it.

The winter was an easy one. There was plenty of food, water, and firewood. The weather was good, too.

Another summer came. When Om's people met their friends that summer, the campfires were filled with stories of elkdogs. Om learned that other Blackfeet warriors and scouts had also seen elkdogs. One group of Blackfeet warriors had been attacked by Snake warriors riding on the backs of elkdogs.

They told stories about the elkdog's speed. No man could run from elkdogs. The enemy rides swiftly, shoots his arrows, and is gone before Blackfeet warriors have a good chance to shoot their arrows.

In late summer two Blackfeet hunters came into camp with the most exciting story of all. They said they saw two enemy hunters ride their elkdogs next to a herd of buffalo. While the elkdog ran stride for stride with the stampeding buffalo, the hunter shot his arrows into one of the great beasts until it fell. Each rider killed two buffalo this way in a very short time.

While the Blackfeet men watched from their hiding place, they saw women come and cut up the animals. When the work was done, more women came. Each was leading an elkdog. The Blackfeet watched as huge loads of meat and hides were tied to the backs of the horses. Soon the enemy people were gone with all four buffalo.

This story was also repeated many times the rest of the summer. Om and Twin Girl listened to every word. Never in their young lives had anything more exciting happened. They knew they too might see elkdogs any day.

Because of the danger of meeting the enemy warriors who rode elkdogs, the Blackfeet people decided to find a new winter camp in a valley farther to the east. The long trip to winter camp was made very carefully. Scouts ran farther and worked harder than ever to find the enemy and avoid a surprise attack.

When the people came to the place where the three waters meet, they turned east and traveled through the wide valley toward the mountains. They passed the site where Bozeman, Montana, is today and made their way over a pass to a new valley. A large river flows from this valley and is called the Yellowstone River today.

Om's people turned south and followed the river up the valley. At a safe place they crossed to the east side. The valley was very wide where the crossing was made.

The leaders kept the people moving toward a tall mountain peak on the east. This mountain is almost eleven thousand feet high. Today it is called Emigrant Peak.

The people and even the dogs were excited when their new winter campsite was found. The place chosen was a creekbed next to the mountains. This creek flowed out of the mountains and had cut out a nice low campsite protected from the winds. There are homesites there today on Mill Creek.

This new valley was strange to all the Blackfeet people. Nothing looked familiar. There was plenty of firewood and clear cold water. There were many fresh signs of moose, elk, and deer.

Camp was made near the creek in a small meadow protected by aspen, pine, and spruce trees. Lodges were put up in places to take advantage of level ground and the trees.

It was late fall when the campsite was found. The high mountains were already snow-covered. In the valley patches of snow covered the ground where trees shaded it from the sun.

Om was busy helping clear a site for his family lodge. Travois poles were used along with newly cut poles to make the cone-shaped frame. With a snug hide covering, the lodge would be small but cozy. The dogs and people could not carry enough hides to make a bigger tepee. During the day the hides that made the beds were folded back from the center of the lodge. This made room for a fire in the center of the tepee. Fir wood that caused very little smoke was burned. The little smoke there was traveled on the rising heat waves to an opening in the top of the tepee. Only a small fire was needed to warm the tiny lodge.

Besides the hides, the dogs had carried dried meat, roots, and berries on the long trip south. Most of the food was buried in the ground to keep it safe from small animals. Holes were dug near the lodges. Baskets woven from reeds were lined with willow twigs. After they were filled with dried food, the baskets were placed in the holes, covered with twigs and grass, and then buried under a foot or more of soil.

Large piles of firewood were gathered by the women and children. The men left every day in search of game.

They hoped this valley would be as good for hunting as was the valley the people had used in past winters.

At first this new winter camp was perfect. The weather was beautiful. The hunting was excellent. Everything seemed to be better than ever.

Then about the middle of winter things changed. The weather turned bitter cold. Strong winds and blowing snow made hunting almost impossible. One day a hunter was lost. He fell and broke his hip. Before he was found, his toes and fingers were badly frozen. His ability as a hunter was ruined.

Without fresh meat, much of the supply of dried food had to be eaten. Now each person could have only a small portion of the normal amount of daily food. Many days the people huddled in their lodges to keep warm while the bitter cold winds howled through the valley.

Om helped his father build a wall of logs around their lodge to keep the wind and blowing snow away. They put the log poles on end into the snow. This made a strong wall that was more than eight feet high. Snow was piled high against the wall to close off all the cracks.

Om loved to build things. Many times he stood back and looked at the wall. It made him feel good inside. It made him want to do more work just like it.

Soon the boy was building a wall for Old Man. Om loved the old man. His stories were the best of all. His wisdom was great. Om always remembered that it was Old Man who had told the other men that Om's mother should be allowed to keep her twin babies when they were born. The boy remembered the story well. Old Man had said, "Let the days ahead give us our wisdom."

Om knew that these words gave his mother the chance to prove to everyone that her great love for her babies helped her do more work than ever and not become a burden. Tall Woman had earned the right to keep Om and Twin Girl. All of his life Om would work hard to prove that the people were right in allowing him and his sister, Twin Girl, to live.

As the bitter cold weather continued, the people became more miserable. Food supplies were very low. Hunters could not travel far from the camp. Blowing snow blinded them. Hunting was impossible.

Om had heard Old Man tell stories about hard winters he knew as a boy. Men with special powers went into their lodges alone and sat for hours, even days, asking the spirits to lead their hunters to meat. Old Man said that one winter the people became so hungry they ate some of their hide clothing to keep from starving. He said he saw some of this people become so weak that the death spirits took them while they slept.

Would this winter end in death for some of Om's people? Would Speaks-With-Spirits' prayers for a good hunt work? All Om heard about was the bad weather, the need for food, and the troubles of his people.

The boy had very little to feed Wise Bird. Anything the raven was given had to come from Om's own food supply. Tall Woman told him not to give the bird any of his food. She said ravens are able to go for many days without any food at all. She told him to eat his food himself to keep up his strength. But it was impossible for the boy to eat and not give his friend something. The raven's little black eyes watched the boy's every move while he ate.

Suddenly after many days the raging storm let up. Now the hunters had their chance. Their sharpened spears and bows and arrows were ready. They pulled on their winter moccasins and winter clothes and set out on the hunt. The day was clear and very cold, but there was no wind.

Looking west across the valley, Om could see rolling hills. These slopes had few trees and were windblown. There was hardly any snow on them. In many places there was bare ground. Deer, elk, and other grass-eating animals looked for these windblown places. Here they could find feed, so they had a chance of surviving the long hard winters.

The hunters knew the animals' habits. Their hunt would begin on those distant slopes. Because there were few trees and bushes to hide the hunters, getting close enough for a shot would be very difficult.

The long trip across the valley meant crossing the big river. The crossing was made over a place where the water was deep and slow-moving. In these places thick ice covered the river. Hunters wanted to cross without getting wet. Staying dry in the freezing cold was a must.

Frozen feet would be a tragedy for any Blackfeet hunter. His ability to run at top speed for long distances was often the only way he could make a kill.

Om ran to a high place above the camp to watch the hunters move west. He wished he could go. Maybe they would need him to come and help carry a load of meat back to the village. The boy was hungry enough to eat raw meat. As Om stood thinking about the taste of fresh meat, Wise Bird flew from a nearby aspen tree and landed on the boy's shoulder. Om absentmindedly stroked the raven's back. Wise Bird began pecking at the boy's hair. This was what the bird did when he wanted Om's attention.

"What is it, Wise Bird? What do you want? I know you're hungry. Why don't you find some food for me? I too am hungry."

No sooner had Om finished speaking than the huge raven launched itself into the air and flew off to the south. Wise Bird flew in a wide circle, then south again. The raven made a second circle and then went farther south.

Om watched his raven curiously. Wise Bird flew the same pattern as he had on the day he found the lost baby.

"What are you doing, Wise Bird? Now what have you found?"

"Why don't you go and see?"

The boy turned to see who asked such a question. There stood Twin Girl. She had a large load of firewood.

Om had no answer at first. Then he said, "Yes, I will. I will go and see what feast the wise raven has found for us."

All hunters that kill game are surprised at how fast ravens, coyotes, eagles, and magpies come to share in the kill. It is almost as if one of them smells the feast and quickly goes to tell his family and friends. Maybe Wise Bird knew something. Om would go to find out what his secret was.

The boy began his walk south, staying on the high open ground. Here there was little snow, and walking was easy. Om kept his eyes on Wise Bird as the raven flew so smoothly in great circles, always moving south a little farther.

Om hiked for a long time. Sometimes he ran to catch up with Wise Bird. He had to slow down when he came into deep snow. He was weaker than usual. He was very hungry. That morning the boy had shared what little he had to eat with his raven.

I hope Wise Bird is leading me to food. Maybe he knows where there has been a winter kill of a moose or a buffalo. I wonder what secret he has for me, Om thought.

Om's thoughts kept his mind off his hunger. He hardly took time to stop for a rest. Something told him to keep going. It seemed that Wise Bird had started to fly in smaller and smaller circles. Soon the raven was not flying south at all. He just circled over the same place.

Om began to catch up with the great bird. The boy had been led far from his village. The day was half over. The weather was still clear and very cold. The sun was bright on the white blanket of snow. Om's eyes were fastened on Wise Bird now flying high above him. He did not pay much attention to anything else around him.

The boy had stopped to wait for the raven's next move. He glanced around the slope he had just crossed.

Straight ahead he could see a high mountain rising far above the lower ridges near it. There were no trees on the highest part of this beautiful peak. It seemed to stand by itself against the bright blue sky. The mountain seemed to be very close to the boy. Om knew it was really quite a distance from him. He noticed a gap between a hill on the west and the mountains he was traveling next to. The gap led around to the great peak.

On one of his circles Wise Bird suddenly banked sharply and flew straight toward the gap that Om had just been studying. The raven was flying at top speed, no more lazy circles. The boy sensed that something was about to happen. He started running as fast as he could through the snow. This run made him feel very tired. As he slowed to a walk, he lost sight of the raven.

The boy kept walking. He was crossing a bench-like hill that ran south just above the valley floor. Om didn't see Wise Bird, but he could hear the raven's familiar call. It was the call Wise Bird made when he was most excited. He had used this same call when he found the lost baby.

Om knew the sound was coming from the left. He entered a thick grove of spruce trees to his left. The spruce branches had caught most of the snow so the ground beneath them was almost bare. Walking was easy except where branches crossed each other and blocked Om's way.

Wise Bird's call sounded louder and louder with every step the boy took. Om knew the raven was just ahead. Soon I'll know why Wise Bird has led me all this way, thought Om. I'm so hungry. It has to be food. I'm so hungry. Many thoughts rushed through the weary boy's mind.

When Om came out of the trees, he saw the raven perched on the branch of a dead spruce tree. This tree was on the opposite side of a small meadow. The whole opening was surrounded by trees.

Om started straight for Wise Bird's tree. The going was slow in the deep snow. The boy was in it up to his knees most of the way.

As Om neared the tree where Wise Bird waited, he came to a sight which made his heart sink. There in the snow lay the badly-torn body of a large snowshoe rabbit.

"Oh, no! Wise Bird, is this why you led me to this far place? The coyote that killed this rabbit has eaten most of it. This is a bad thing. Why did you do this to me? How can I ever follow you again?"

Om's words were filled with disappointment. He felt so let down. All this way, all that energy, all that time, and all for the scrawny carcass of a rabbit. Finally all Om could say was, "Well, Wise Bird, I guess you did your best." In his misery that was the best the boy could do.

6

A Secret Revealed

Om felt let down as he knelt to pick up what was left of the mangled rabbit. At least he would have a little to chew on and a little meat to take back to his family.

While he was gathering up the remains of the rabbit Om's ears caught a strange sound. It was a muffled thumping sound. As he listened the sound stopped. In a few minutes it started again.

Om stood up, and Wise Bird swooped down and landed on his shoulder. The raven let out one loud squawk and took off. The big bird flew to the south end of the meadow, rose above the trees, and circled around, waiting for the boy to follow.

Om dropped the rabbit, kicked snow over it until it was safely hidden, and ran after Wise Bird. First the strange sound, and now the raven wants me to follow him again. What does all this mean?

The boy was excited again. He stopped at the edge of the meadow and listened. At first there was only silence. Suddenly this stillness was broken by a loud thumping sound. Om headed right for the sound. This time when the thumping sound stopped, the boy could hear heavy breathing. Om took a few more steps toward the sound. His eyes saw a movement through the trees and straight ahead.

Om came to a small opening in the trees. There, just a short distance from him, the boy saw a huge bull elk. Its head was down and its hind legs were stiff and straight. When Om got a little closer, he saw that the elk's large set of antlers was caught in the twisted roots of a fallen tree. The majestic animal had been trapped there for hours. In its struggle for freedom, the big bull had pawed a hole more than two feet deep in the frozen ground. Its front hooves were bloody and worn from all the digging. Lather dripped from the big elk's body. The creature had spent most of its strength in the desperate attempt to escape. Now the terrified animal rested longer and longer between its struggles to get free.

The elk was one of the largest Om had ever seen. The boy had to act fast. This animal was food for his people. He could not let it get away. There was no time to go for help. He would have to kill the trapped animal by himself. Om could see that if the elk moved forward at just the right angle, it might get free. The boy couldn't let that happen. The only weapon Om had was a knife. It would be too dangerous to try to kill an animal this large with just a small knife. The boy made his plans. He quickly pulled a large dead branch from a tree. His hands moved fast as he began sharpening one end of this branch. His stone-point knife made the work go slowly.

Working as fast as he could, Om was making good progress. Then his troubles began. The stone point came loose from its cottonwood handle. The boy pushed the point back in place. Quickly he tied another hide thong around the handle to hold the point in place. It was still quite loose. The work was very slow now. Om worked on frantically.

Several times the big elk pulled, pawed, and strained to get free. Its front legs churned at the rocky frozen ground. The huge bull breathed loudly and made desperate sounds deep in his throat. Every time the elk renewed his struggle, Om worked even faster. He stayed out of sight so the beast would not see him and try even harder in his effort to escape.

With the loose knife point, Om's work seemed to be taking forever. He wondered if he could ever finish in time. He had to. He could not let this great elk escape. This animal would be hundreds of pounds of meat for his people. It might even save some lives.

The boy worked feverishly. His fingers were cold and sore. In some places his skin had been worn through and was bleeding. The loose knife point made things miserable.

When Om finally had the end of the branch sharp enough, he had to plan the best way to use it to kill the elk. The branch was thick and should not break. The boy knew the lower part of the elk's neck was the best spot for the spear to strike. He would probably be able to strike just one blow with the spear. His knife would have to do the rest. Now he was ready.

The boy's heart pounded as he thought through his plan step by step. He would move quickly to a place close to the animal's head right after it stopped for a rest. Before the animal knew what was happening, Om would use every ounce of his strength to make a fatal wound in its huge neck. If he could pull the spear free, he would make another strike. The boy had his knife ready, but would use it only if he had to.

The great elk made its last frantic fight to free itself and stood still in total exhaustion. Instantly Om ran forward with his spear. Before the terrified animal could move, the boy used all his strength to strike a mighty blow with the spear. His aim was perfect. The spear hit a vital artery, and the huge bull struggled for only a few seconds, collapsed, and died.

It was all over so fast that Om could not believe how easy it was. Still the boy stayed well back as the animal was dying. He would make sure the elk was dead before getting too close. His father had told him about eager

hunters who were badly injured by animals they thought
were dead. Never get close until you are sure it's safe,
Otterman had said. Om used this wise advice as he
stood catching his breath.

The events of this day used up many hours. Winter
days are short. By the time Om had the animal all
cleaned out, it would be dark. The boy had to work fast.
Then he needed a plan for saving the meat and hide.
Somehow he had to get help in getting it all back to his
people.

Cleaning the large elk was slow work with a knife with
a loose point. The warmth of the animal's body felt good
on Om's cold hands. When the boy reached the liver, he
quickly cut pieces off for himself and Wise Bird. The raw
meat was warm and tender. It tasted delicious and
renewed Om's strength. It would help him do all the
work that was ahead.

The sun dipped below the hills in the west as Om finished cleaning out the elk. There was no time to make it
back to his village by dark. If he left the elk all night,
wolves, coyotes, eagles, ravens, and magpies would help
themselves and eat much of it. The ground was frozen

solid. Om couldn't bury the meat. He knew he would have to stay all night right next to the elk. He would need shelter to survive the bitter cold night.

Om had several choices for a shelter. He could dig a snow cave. He could build a small shelter with spruce boughs. He even remembered stories of hunters sleeping inside the bodies of freshly killed animals. One way or another the boy knew he would survive the below-zero cold.

For the first time since he saw the great elk, Om took a look around to see exactly where he was. With Wise Bird on his shoulder, the boy walked out of the trees to an open slope for a better view.

A great bald eagle was already circling above the kill. Coyotes called to each other in the distance.

In the fading light Om noticed a column of steam coming from the ground below him and to his left. Often water vapor rose from creeks and rivers during winter, making banks of fog over the land. This thick mist was coming from only one spot. The boy also noticed a familiar smell in the air.

Wise Bird took to the air as Om ran toward the column of steam. When he stopped running the boy was standing beside a spring of very hot water gurgling out of the rocks. Om knelt and put his hand into the warm water. He had seen other hot springs and knew their smells. He also knew how good they were for people.

Now Om had a plan. He looked toward the trees where the elk lay. Yes, he could pull the elk down the hill over the snow to the hot spring. He would skin the animal and use the hide to make a shelter near the hot water. The next day he would run to his village for help.

Om raced back to the elk. Two magpies were already pecking at the meat. They flew off when he got near.

It was a long hard struggle to get the elk the short distance downhill to the spring. Om left the head and the antlers, which were still tangled in the roots. He pulled the rest of the huge animal by its front legs. He could pull it only a few feet at a time. He rested by sitting on the warm carcass. Then the boy was up again to pull for a few more feet. There were several fallen trees and big rocks to go around. Om was getting worn out from his long hard day.

When the tired boy finally pulled the elk the last few feet to the spring, he sat on the body with Wise Bird at his side. They both enjoyed some more raw liver.

"Wise Bird, you did have a big secret. You are a great raven. Our people will hear the story of your discovery. You earned you food today!"

The raven turned his head from side to side as Om spoke. The boy wondered how much the bird could understand.

As Om ate, he planned his final tasks of the day. He had to skin the elk and build a lean-to with the hide. The flap to the lean-to would go over the hot spring. The warm water would heat the shelter enough to keep the boy from freezing.

It took a long time to skin the large animal in the dark. Om took more time to repair the knife. The point came loose only once during the skinning work.

When the hide was finally free from the elk's body, Om quickly made a frame for his lean-to. When it was done the shelter had a floor and was closed in on both sides. The front opening was only two feet high. The overhang caught the heat from the hot spring.

The boy crawled in and got as comfortable as he could. The warmth from the hot water felt good, but Om soon felt damp all over. The side of his body facing the spring was warm. The side facing the back of the lean-to soon got very cold. All night he kept turning over often to keep both sides of his body warm. He would survive the night but he would not sleep very much. When he did doze off, he would soon awaken and feel ice forming on the side of his body that was not facing the hot water.

This hot spring is now called Chico Hot Springs. Today it is a wonderful resort. For Om it was a place to survive a long, miserable night, but survive he did.

At first light the next day, Om crawled from his lean-to. He crouched down as close to the hot spring as he could. Om took out a piece of frozen elk liver and chewed on it. Wise Bird landed at his feet for his share of meat. The boy had put some of the liver in the hot water to thaw. He cut some pieces of it for his raven.

During the night, Om had made his plan for this day. He would bury the elk meat as deeply as possible in the snow. Then he planned to run nonstop back to his village. Time was important. If he was gone too long wolves or coyotes would uncover the meat and have a feast. If only someone were here to help me, he thought.

While the boy worked hard to bury the elk meat, Wise Bird disappeared. Om put the last bit of snow on the pile, turned, and began running for home as fast as he could. Om was still damp all over from staying so close to the steaming hot spring. In minutes his long black hair began to freeze. Frost formed on his eyebrows. Icicles hung from his buckskin suit. Inside his body stayed warm as he ran steadily toward home.

Om hadn't gone far when he looked up and saw Wise Bird flying straight toward him.

"There you are, Wise Bird. Where did you go?"

The boy slowed to a jogging pace as he spoke to his pet raven. Wise Bird just circled over Om. His large wings caught the air currents as he soared overhead.

Om paid no more attention to the raven. He kept his eyes on his route. Every minute counted. He must get to the camp without delay.

The boy picked up speed and ran on for another mile. Coming up on a hillside, he could see far ahead. It looked like something was moving on the snow. In a short time he could see it was a runner coming his way. The runner looked small. It couldn't be a man.

Om ran even faster. As he came over a small rise, he saw this lone runner below him. It was Twin Girl! She dashed up the hill to meet him.

When Twin Girl got close to Om, she stopped some distance from him. There was a shocked look on her face. Om looked strange. She hardly recognized her own brother. His hair was solid ice. His eyebrows were thick with frost. His clothes were frosty white and snapped and cracked when he moved. Twin Girl had never seen such a sight. She wondered what strange place he had come from. What had happened to him there? He looked like a creature from the spirit world.

"Twin Girl! It's you. You have come to help. How did you know?" Om's words came between his gasps for air.

"Om-kas-toe! What has happened to you? You are covered with ice. What strange place have you visited? Wise Bird came to the village and led me here."

Quickly Om told his story about Wise Bird, the rabbit, the great elk, and the hot spring.

"Twin Girl, follow my trail to the elk. Wait there. I will return with our hunters."

Before the girl could answer, Om was running again. The boy made the run to the village at a pace faster than he had ever run in his life. Like Twin Girl, all the people stared at Om and wondered what strange place he had visited. Some thought he had fallen into the river on his way home.

Om told about the elk while he warmed himself by the fire. Before he left to lead the hunters back to the elk, he changed buckskins. His rest was very short. Now he turned and ran off, leading the hunters to the hot spring. The boy and four men were followed by four women with dogs and travois for carrying the meat.

It was a long, tiring day for Om, but he even remembered to stop and pick up the parts of the buried rabbit. Every little bit of meat would help. The people returned to the village with all of the elk that day. There was great joy in the camp.

Twin Girl told Om she knew he would survive, because the night he was gone she had had a special dream. It was a dream she had had many times before. In the dream she and Om each were riding an elkdog over their favorite trails.

The morning Twin Girl got up and Om had not returned yet, she went out of the lodge and found Wise Bird waiting for her. The raven landed on her head and pecked at the bone in her hair. Then the great bird took off, flying south. Twin Girl left the village and soon picked up Om's tracks. The rest the boy knew.

The elk meat came just in time. The hunters had shot no game at all. Each family was given a fair share. Not one scrap was wasted. Even the bone marrow was removed from the center of the bones and eaten. The tongue was a favorite piece of meat and went to Om's family. They got the hide, also.

The story of Wise Bird's secret was one of the best his people had ever heard. Om was praised for his skill and good thinking in the kill of the elk. The discovery of the hot spring was a wonderful thing. As soon as possible, the people built a small pool to hold the hot water. A soak in it would be good medicine for their bodies. Hides were sewn together to cover a small pool of the hot water, creating a great sweatbath.

Two days after Om's return the hunters killed a
moose and her yearling calf. These two animals pro-
duced a great supply of meat and hides. From this time
on hunting was much better and the signs of spring
promised an end to a very hard winter.

7

Twin Girl's Amazing Discovery

Springtime in this new valley was the best Om had ever known. Hunting was excellent. There was always a good supply of fresh meat. Much of it was eaten after being roasted over open fires.

Best of all for Om, he was taken on many of the hunts. He was only a helper and never got close enough to make a kill. The boy was happy and filled with great excitement every minute of the hunts.

The boy's legs and lungs became stronger than ever. He could run faster than any boy his age. He could even run as fast as some men. He hoped that someday he could run as fast as that great warrior, Runs-Like-Antelope. Om was always amazed to see this mighty hunter run at top speed through the sagebrush. The boy often looked at Runs-Like-Antelope's powerful legs when the hunter walked through the camp. Someday Om would have legs like this great hunter's. Om planned to be the fastest runner of all when he became a man.

The leaders watched the great river closely. A crossing would have to be made before the melting snows filled the river with swift water. Dogs and people would have to be on the other side before the high waters came.

After much talk, it was decided that the winter camp would be broken and a temporary camp set up across the river. Om was not as excited as usual to leave the winter camp. He had had some great adventures at this place. It also meant leaving the hot spring that he had discovered on that exciting day.

Twin Girl's favorite dog was all trained to pull a travois. Thunder was the most tame and gentle dog in the whole village. The girl had spent many hours with this dog. She kept him away from the other dogs most of the time.

Thunder was a large dog but not the largest. His face was black. His body was a light tan color with black hairs sprinkled through his thick coat. His eyes were always on Twin Girl, waiting for her next signal or move. The friendly dog still let Wise Bird sit on his back at any time. Twin Girl, Om, Wise Bird, and Thunder were often seen together enjoying a meal.

Even the dogs seemed less excited about leaving this winter camp. Maybe they sensed that this first move would be a short one.

Camp was set up west of the big river after a quick and easy crossing through shallow water. The new camp was not nearly as good as the old one but would be fine until the trip north began.

Hunting was still very good, and Om had many chances to go with the men. He learned the importance of seeing the game animals before they saw him. This gave the hunter a good chance to get close enough for a shot with bow and arrow. If the first shot missed, the hunter probably would not get a second chance.

During one of the hunts, Om saw Wise Bird far ahead, circling over a section of a creek. The boy reached out and tapped his father's arm. When Otterman looked at Om, the boy pointed at the raven gracefully circling high to the right of the hunters.

Otterman silently motioned to three hunters nearby. He signaled them to follow him. Staying low, the hunters moved to the right. They went flat on their stomachs as they reached the top of a small rise. Their eyes searched the creek bottom below where they lay. The willows were thick and tall. New spring growth would begin soon.

The hunter on the far left was the first to see something moving in the thick willows. With hand signs he sent a silent message to the others. Two giant bull moose were right below him. The animals did not know the hunters were so close.

Moose have poor eyesight and can be stalked easily. They are dangerous, though. A moose can kill a man with one blow of its sharp hooves.

While the hunters moved closer, Om was sent to get more men. He was to tell them the direction of the attack and what they should do to help bring down these two huge moose.

The hunt was easy. The hunters got close enough to use their spears. These two animals added hundreds of pounds of meat to the village supply. The hides were valuable.

Once again the boy and his raven had found game animals. Again Om was the center of attention. At the evening campfire the leaders asked many questions about Wise Bird. Om-kas-toe, can you send the raven out to hunt any time you wish? How do you speak to the bird? Does Wise Bird speak to you?

Om's answers were always the same and amazed the people. He told them the raven was a special gift to him and his Blackfeet people. Yes, Wise Bird did listen to Om. In its own way, the raven understood all people. The bird understood people who understood him.

Om's answers added mystery to an already fascinating story of a boy and his special raven.

Time to move north came two weeks after the moose hunt. With dogs barking, people tying packs to the travois, and children putting packs over their shoulders and onto their backs, it was a time of great excitement.

The men spread out in front of and all around the moving line of people and dogs. They would be on the lookout for the enemy that might come riding elkdogs.

The people moved north, downriver, to the place where the valley narrowed. After passing this narrow place, Om's people made camp for the night on the site of the present-day city of Livingston, Montana. Here the leaders talked about which route to follow the next day. To the west they would be closer to their enemies. To the east they would travel strange lands but be farther from their enemies who had elkdogs.

In the end the men decided to go west over a pass and travel to the place where the three waters meet to form the great river. Here they would move quickly to the west side of the place where the waters meet. From there they would move north, keeping their distance from the great river. Extra guards at night and extra scouts during the day would help make travel safe.

Today Interstate 90 follows the route Om's people would take over Bozeman Pass and on to Three Forks.

Then they would head north along what is now Highway 287 toward Helena, Montana.

The leaders of the Blackfeet knew the Snake warriors would soon be coming into these valleys to hunt. Each day the Blackfeet leaders made the people travel faster and farther. The long hard days began to wear the people out. At night people and dogs ate and went right to sleep. No shelters were put up. When rains came, hides were used to cover the sleeping people. Often water seeped under the hides, and the people woke up cold and wet.

As the weary band of Blackfeet moved north far west of the great river, they arrived in a wide valley. It stretched many miles north toward high mountain ridges. Om's people had traveled this way many times in the past. To avoid the enemy they stayed much farther west of the great river than usual.

It was late afternoon when camp was made. The leaders said lodges could be put up. Camp would be made here for several days. The men were sure the enemy would not come near this place this early in the summer. Now there would be time to rest, time to repair travois, and even time to hunt. Guards and scouts would be alert for signs of the enemy.

Om and Twin Girl were happy to hear the news. The next day there would be no packing, no walking, no tired dogs to push ahead. It would be a wonderful time for everyone. Even Wise Bird seemed to know the long hard marches were over.

Om was glad to be able to sleep in a lodge again. Let the rain come. Let the dew and the frost settle. The boy slept well knowing he would be warm and dry all night long.

The location of this camp would someday become the site of Helena, Montana. Lodges were well hidden in the trees. No Indian trails came near this campsite. Only a little hunting was done here. The people still had plenty of food. Scouts left each morning to go out in every direction to look for signs of the enemy.

Just when the people were enjoying their stay the most, Runs-Like-Antelope came dashing into the camp. Between deep breaths he spoke loudly: "Enemy warriors—elkdogs—on the trail—near the great river."

The people moved fast. Down came the tepees. Packs were made in a hurry. Dogs were harnessed. The move was on. Blackfeet warriors took their weapons and went out to defend their people.

It was late in the day. The enemy warriors had not seen the Blackfeet scouts or the camp, but they were close enough to make it very dangerous.

Again the people and dogs were moving away from danger. They kept to the trees and willows whenever possible. The warriors did not let the enemy out of their sight. There were more than thirty Snake warriors, all riding horses. If they saw the Blackfeet, there would be a terrible battle. Many would die. Many Blackfeet women and children would be captured.

There was no fight that day. Om's people gave the enemy the slip. Darkness was a big help. From that day on everyone talked about the close call. They talked about the elkdog and how they too needed this animal to ride into battle and to use for hunting. But how could the Blackfeet get elkdogs? No enemy would give them away or even trade them. No, the Blackfeet would have to send a war party to track down the enemy and steal their elkdogs. This would be dangerous but would have to be done.

Om's heart beat fast as he thought about the leaders' words. Follow the enemy, attack them, and steal their elkdogs. Could it be done? What if the enemy followed them? How could a Blackfeet warrior ride an elkdog if he didn't know how? What if he got on an elkdog and it wouldn't run away from the enemy?

The boy's mind went over and over these questions. It was hard to sleep that night wondering about it all.

An early start the next day made the people realize their rest was over. Camp was made early that spring afternoon. A place was picked at the foot of some hills at the north end of this huge valley. Once again lodges were put up in the forest. From the high places on the slopes, guards could see long distances in every direction. The people would be safe here.

Om was busy doing his camp work when his father came up to him. "Come, my son. You will be a guard today. White Wolf will show you where to stand. Use your eyes well, my son. Our people depend on us."

A hunter and now a guard. Om felt very important indeed. His eyes would see well. If the enemy were there, Om would know. He would be quick to warn his people.

White Wolf led Om to a pile of broken rock high on a hill. A large dead tree trunk stood in the center of the rocks. It had been broken off about twenty feet up by a bolt of lightning many years before this time.

From Om's lookout he could see for many miles to the west, the east, and the south. Other guards watched from the north side of this hill.

At first being a guard was exciting. As the hours passed, Om began to get bored. His eyes had searched the same places over and over. Even Wise Bird was not interested. The raven sat on a rock, cleaning his wing feathers and snoozing.

Shadows in the valley got longer as the afternoon went on. Om noticed it was harder to see in this light. He was thinking how much better it was to go hunting.

Om was startled when a boy came around the rocks behind him. This boy had come to take Om's place. After a few words with the boy, Om started downhill toward the camp. He was very hungry and tired. He never dreamed what would happen to him on his way there. No other event would ever mean more to him and his people.

The boy was about halfway back to camp when Wise Bird left his shoulder and swooped down the hill. The raven had spotted Twin Girl digging roots off to the left. She was about one-half mile from the camp.

Om saw Wise Bird glide to the branch of a cotton-wood tree just above Twin Girl's head. He saw his sister was digging roots. Then he saw her suddenly drop all her roots and crouch down behind a bush. Twin Girl was looking away from Om. She stayed very still as if she were suddenly turned to stone.

Om stopped. He tried to see what caused Twin Girl to act so strangely. Maybe she saw the enemy or an animal to hunt. Something scared her.

Slowly Twin Girl turned to face Om. She raised her hand and motioned to Om to stay low and to come to her.

Quickly the boy crouched as low as he could and began moving toward Twin Girl. His heart beat faster. He

had to be careful not to step on any dry twigs or to kick any rocks loose.

Why was Twin Girl acting this way? What did she see? Did danger wait beyond the bushes where the girl was hidden? Many thoughts went through Om's mind. It seemed to take a long time to cover such a short distance.

When Om got to Twin Girl, she was on her knees peering over the bushes that hid her so well. She said nothing. Her left hand raised slowly, and she pointed over the bush.

At first when Om looked over the bush, he saw nothing special. There was only a long open slope covered with thick green grass and wildflowers. That was all he could see until he raised up a little more. Now he could see what made Twin Girl so excited. What he saw made his mouth go dry. There not more than a short walk away stood an elkdog. The horse had a rope hanging from its neck and just stood grazing quietly on the lush grass.

An elkdog! Here! Where is the enemy? He must be near. What should I do? I'll run and tell our people!

Then Om remembered the words and lessons of his father. "Before you do anything, wait, think, plan, and then do what you think is best for your people. Never do the first thing you think of."

Om and Twin Girl could not take their eyes off this beautiful animal. They had a perfect place to watch its every move without being seen. While Om watched he made his plan of what to do next. He hoped it would be the right thing to do. It just had to be.

8

Capturing Elkdog

Om decided the first thing he should do was to find out if any enemy warriors were close by. This would be the greatest danger to his people. The boy used sign language to tell Twin Girl to stay and keep her eyes on elkdog while he did his scouting work. He would be back soon.

Om planned to go in a great circle around the elkdog to look for any signs of enemy warriors. He would try to stay out of sight as much as possible.

The boy was gone for what seemed to be a long time. His trip took him over some loose rock and through a thick growth of chokecherry bushes. Several times he had to wade through swampy places where water oozed from the mountainside. Om saw no signs of the enemy. He did see the strange tracks of this elkdog. He saw older signs of moose and elk. The boy was sure elkdog had come here alone.

Om still wondered where this elkdog's rider was. How did this animal come to be in this place? What strange things were happening this day?

Twin Girl was glad to see Om return. She was afraid the elkdog would leave before he got back. The beautiful animal was still very close. The twins whispered together as they planned what to do next.

"We must not let this elkdog out of our sight," whispered Om. "If we go for help, elkdog might leave. One of us must stay and watch him. One of us must go to get help."

The twins thought about Om's words. Then Twin Girl said the words her brother seemed ready to say himself.

"Let's capture this elkdog ourselves. He is tame like a dog. He will not run from us. Look how he quietly eats the grass. We can walk up to him just as the enemy does. His rope is there for us to hold like we hold a dog's."

Om wanted to do it, but he wondered, what if elkdog runs away and escapes? What if the two of us are not strong enough to hold the big animal?

Om spoke next. "We can capture elkdog. Twin Girl, you walk from here straight toward elkdog. I will be hiding below him in the bushes. I will keep him from running away downhill. Wait for me to get to my hiding place. Then stand and walk slowly toward elkdog. When you are close, I will stand and walk uphill to elkdog."

As Om whispered his plan to Twin Girl, he spoke as one who had done this same thing in the past. He spoke as if he knew his plan would work perfectly.

In just minutes Om, hidden in a bush, was watching elkdog. Twin Girl was ready. She stood up and began to walk slowly toward the grazing horse. When the animal heard her coming, it raised its head and turned to watch her for several minutes. It was then that Twin Girl began

to sing very softly. She sang a favorite chant her mother
had taught her when she was very young.

Twin Girl walked along as though she was interested
in everything around her. She never looked directly at
the elkdog. She didn't even walk in a straight line. The
horse moved only a few steps the whole time. His move
was made to get to more good grass.

Om could not believe his eyes. Twin Girl was going to
walk right up to elkdog with no problem. The hiding boy
knew he would change his plan. He would not stand up
at all. He would stay hidden. Twin Girl was doing perfectly by herself. Om was not needed. He might startle
the animal by showing himself.

This scene was one Om would never forget. Twin Girl
walked closer and closer. Soon she stood right next to
elkdog while it kept eating. Om could not take his eyes
off this amazing sight.

Twin Girl stood next to the neck of elkdog. She sang
her chant softly as her left hand moved slowly toward
the rope that hung limply from the horse's neck. Then
her fingers touched the braided hide rope. She grasped
it firmly but did not pull on the rope. Twin Girl didn't

know it, but this elkdog was very tired and very hungry. It had carried its rider on a buffalo hunt. In the stampede the horse fell, throwing its rider to his death under the hooves of the huge beasts. The horse was unhurt. It got up and ran many miles. It crossed several low mountain ridges and finally stopped on this hillside.

As Twin Girl held the rope, the elkdog lifted its head and turned to look at the girl. Twin Girl paid no attention. She continued her singing. Elkdog showed no fear and was soon grazing again.

Om wanted to jump up and run to help Twin Girl. He was never more excited in his whole life, but running might ruin everything. The boy knew he had to stay as calm as possible. Twin Girl had taught him a good lesson. When Om stood up, he too began singing the same chant. In minutes the twins were standing together next to the elkdog. Now what should they do? Om had not thought beyond this moment.

Then Om remembered his time on the rock with White Wolf when they saw the three enemies with their elkdogs. These men walked on the ground and led their animals with the ropes around their necks. When they rode their elkdogs, they held the same rope. The boy decided they too could lead an elkdog.

Om motioned to Twin Girl to give him the rope. He took it in his hand and found it was very long. He had to coil it up. It was twenty-five feet long. Why was it so long? The boy did not realize that the rider had had a long rope coiled and tucked in his belt. If he fell from his horse, he could have a chance to grab the rope before the horse got away.

The boy took the coil he had made and moved out in front of elkdog. The animal's head came up. It made a loud breathing sound and pulled back on the rope. Om held the rope tightly and gave a steady pull. Elkdog gave only a little resistance and then took two steps toward the boy. Om turned like a person who had led a horse many times before and, holding the rope firmly, walked forward. The beautiful animal followed him.

Twin Girl walked next to her brother. She turned her head often to watch this amazing animal follow them. This was like a dream. It was hard for Twin Girl to believe that all this was really happening. They had found an elkdog. They had captured an elkdog. The ani-

mal was following them to their camp. It was all too much to believe, but it was really happening.

As the twins walked in front of elkdog, high above them on a ridge two Blackfeet scouts saw them. They could not believe their eyes. They started down the ridge toward this strange scene. The two scouts moved cautiously.

Om and Twin Girl rounded a small grove of trees and came into view of their village. Three small children were the first to see them coming with elkdog. The little ones ran crying to their mothers.

One by one all those in the camp heard the unbelievable news. All work stopped. Everyone in the camp gathered at the edge of the campsite to get a glimpse of this spectacular event.

Before the twins entered the camp, they were met by three men. As these men got close, elkdog stopped. The horse raised its head, pulling Om off balance. The men waited quietly. Elkdog settled down and stood very still again. Soon one of the men walked up to Om and elkdog. Even this warrior was excited and nervous.

The people could see that it was better to stay back and not crowd too close to this strange animal. All was quiet except for soft whispers and murmuring that spread from person to person.

Elkdog was watched closely by every eye in the village. Everything about this animal, even its smell, was new to the people. This elkdog was dark brown with large patches of white all over its body. This horse was small compared to today's horses. Its face was white on one side and dark brown on the other. The long hair on its neck was full of burrs. So was its long tail.

All that afternoon the people spent every spare minute watching every move that the elkdog made. Dogs were kept back so they would not bother this special animal. Twin Girl and Om were allowed to stay close and help hold elkdog's rope.

Men, two or three at a time, came up to elkdog for a closer look. They walked slowly around elkdog. They touched its sides and back. They put a second rope around the animal's neck. It was much stronger. They didn't want elkdog to escape. That night guards would take turns watching elkdog to be sure nothing went wrong.

Om and Twin Girl were the center of attention at a meeting of the whole band that night. They were asked to tell their story of the capture of elkdog. Om was nervous as he spoke, but it was easy to remember every bit of what happened that afternoon. The boy gave Twin Girl most of the credit for it all. He told how she first saw elkdog, and how it was she who had so calmly walked up and captured the huge animal without his help. The boy would never forget any of this story. It would be very real to him the rest of his life.

When Om and Twin Girl finished their stories and answered all the questions, Old Man was the first to stand and speak.

"My children, once again you have been chosen to do a great thing for your people. From the day of your birth the Great Spirit has rewarded the love your mother has shown for you. Not only did you find elkdog, but you were very wise in all that you did. Because of your wisdom and bravery you could capture an elkdog for your people. You brought great honor to your mother, your family, and your people today."

The other leaders followed with short speeches. Some mentioned the gift of Wise Bird, the saving of the lost baby, and the discovery of the bull elk by the hot spring. It was truly a wonderful night for the twins. Otterman and Tall Woman were proud of their special children.

Om and Twin Girl wondered about all that was said. The good feelings they had seemed to fill their entire bodies. That summer their story would be told at campfires all across the open lands. Other Blackfeet bands would listen in amazement to all that was told. They would flock to get a close look at the elkdog. This story of the twins, the raven, and the elkdog would be the favorite around Blackfeet campfires for many years to come.

9

Great Fortune and Sorrow

The high excitement of having an elkdog in the camp went on for days. Still the people had their work to do. They had to continue their journey north to the open lands. Dogs needed packing, loads were still carried by women and children, and warriors were out watching for the enemy.

There was time each day to learn more about elkdog. On the second day elkdog had been in the camp, a warrior lifted himself onto the animal's back while another man held the rope. Elkdog remained quiet and let the man sit on its back. Everyone watched from a distance as elkdog was led in a circle with the man on its back. All were amazed at what elkdog could do. No one talked about anything else.

Every man waited eagerly for a chance to ride elkdog. Younger warriors wanted to ride elkdog by themselves. They didn't want anyone to lead elkdog. Their eagerness worried the older men. We will wait until we know the animal better, was their decision. They did not want anything to go wrong and cause them to lose such an amazing animal.

Each day the people were on the trail with their dogs, a warrior was picked to lead the elkdog. He followed the last dog a safe distance back. At the campsite each night, the men took turns riding elkdog. They went a little farther each ride. They began talking about how they could get elkdog to carry a load. They remembered the story the hunters told of how the Snake women loaded buffalo meat on their elkdogs.

To put a pack on elkdog the men knew the animal would have to have a harness like their dogs had. It would have to be made to fit this huge animal. It would not be easy to make it just right the first time. The elkdog's body was much different from the dogs'.

After much experimenting and long hours of work, the women finally had made a hide harness that fit elkdog perfectly. They had to hold elkdog tightly when they tried to put the harness on him. The animal did not like the harness at all. It fit but there was something wrong. Elkdog let them know about it by his actions.

As the women talked, they decided to use less hide on the harness. Maybe the hide rubbed against the elkdog's body in the wrong places. The women cut much of the hide away, leaving wide bands to form the new harness.

They also made it so they could put it on without having to pull it over elkdog's head. With each improvement, elkdog became less uneasy and more willing to wear the harness. After many days and many hours, the women had a harness that elkdog could wear. Loads could be tied to it easily. Soon elkdog was carrying loads three or four times the size a dog could carry.

When Om's people got to the open lands and met the first Blackfeet people from other bands, the elkdog was the center of attention. Seeing the loads carried by elkdog and watching a young warrior ride the beautiful animal were sights the people never tired of seeing.

Now all the men could talk about was how to get more of these amazing animals. How could they get them? Their enemies would never give them away or even trade for them. The only way the Blackfeet could get more elkdogs would be to take them from the enemy. This would be dangerous. It could not be done during an open battle. Many Blackfeet warriors would lose their lives. It must be done by surprise when the enemy was not aware of an attack.

Around many campfires that summer the leaders of the bands met in council. They talked about how to find the enemy. They planned how they could sneak into the Snake camp and drive the elkdogs away. First each man that went on such a raid must learn to ride elkdog. They would have to rope an elkdog and ride him away to escape.

After much talk and careful planning, a group of six of the strongest and fastest runners were chosen to go on a raid. They would take a supply of dried food, bow and arrows, a spear, and a knife. Also, each man took a rope with which to catch an elkdog. They would never be able to steal the animals and escape on foot.

The six men spent many hours riding the one elkdog that Om and Twin Girl had captured. Without this elkdog to practice with the men would not have a very good chance of success. This elkdog was well behaved and easy to ride. As all good horsemen know, there is a lot of difference in the way each horse behaves. Some are easy to manage and do not scare or spook easily. Other horses can be hard to handle. The least little movement or noise can cause them to rear, buck, or run wildly. The elkdog the Blackfeet had was an outstanding animal for any purpose.

Of the six warriors chosen to go on the elkdog raid, only Runs-Like-Antelope was from Om's band. How the boy wished he could go on this exciting adventure, too.

It was early summer when the six men left the Blackfeet villages for Snake Indian country. They were gone for almost three weeks. Everyone was anxious for their return. Wives of the men talked about their husbands each day. The longer they were gone the more the women worried. The leaders met in council and talked about sending scouts to find out what had happened to these six brave warriors.

One hot afternoon in July a hunter stood on a hill in the shade of a clump of aspen trees. There was no breeze. Only a few puffy white clouds dotted the blue sky. The hunter was on the lookout for buffalo. He strained his eyes to look at a small cloud of dust in the distance. At first he thought the dust was made by a small herd of buffalo. They were coming directly toward him. He waited before giving the signal to other hunters. The animals were moving swiftly.

In just minutes the hunter saw a thrilling sight. These animals were not buffalo. They were elkdogs, a herd of twenty. Right behind them rode five warriors.

The hunter ran for the camp, shouting, "Our men have returned! They have elkdogs, many elkdogs!"

The man's news sent a bolt of excitement through the camps. People dropped everything and rushed to get a look at the elkdogs galloping toward their villages.

The frightened elkdogs came running right into the camps, nearly trampling on some of the people. The men herding them were not used to handling large groups of

elkdogs. They had a hard enough time stopping the elk-dogs they rode.

As the galloping animals came into the camp and slowed to a walk, they were still frightened. Some of them kicked over cooking fires and equipment. Some stepped on hides and knocked over racks of drying meat.

One by one the elkdogs calmed down enough for ropes to be put around their necks. A corral was hurriedly made. It was a temporary one until a more permanent one could be built to hold these large animals.

When the hunter had seen only five riders coming in behind the elkdogs, the people thought one of their warriors had been killed or captured in the raid. Everyone was relieved to see that one elkdog carried two riders. A warrior had ridden all those miles sitting behind Runs-Like-Antelope. He was hanging on with only one arm. The whole story would be told that night.

A great celebration took place around a huge camp-fire. It lasted far into the night. There was dancing and singing and of course the story of the raid was told several times. Runs-Like-Antelope told about the long journey west. They saw the Snake enemy several times before they had a chance to make a surprise raid.

The enemy was camped in a beautiful meadow near a meandering creek. Their elkdogs grazed on the thick grass about three hundred yards from the sleeping warriors. There was one guard that night.

The Blackfeet waited until they saw the first signs of dawn in the eastern sky. A fog in the valley near the creek was perfect to help hide the raiders. Five men crawled on their stomachs toward the elkdogs. One man stalked up on the guard and knocked him out with a perfect tomahawk throw.

The men got close to the elkdogs without a sound. When they all stood up at once to catch an elkdog, the animals whinnied and jumped aside. Five of the Blackfeet roped elkdogs and jumped on them to ride away. The sixth man picked an elkdog that reared high up in the air on its back legs. The warrior was thrown to the ground and broke his right arm. Runs-Like-Antelope saw him fall. He also saw enemy warriors running toward him in the early morning light. Still he jumped from his elkdog and helped the injured man onto his elkdog.

Runs-Like-Antelope jumped on too, and they rode off with arrows being shot right past them by the charging enemy warriors.

Om listened to every word of their story as each man told his part. How he wished he could have been there. The boy enjoyed the whole party. He had never seen such joy and excitement in his whole life.

The next day the men spent all their time with the newly captured elkdogs. There were now twenty-six of these great animals in the possession of the Blackfeet people. They had learned much from the elkdog the twins had captured. They still had much more to learn.

The men took turns riding each of these elkdogs. Some had trouble getting elkdogs to go where they wanted them to go. Some were even thrown by the big stallions. They learned that five of the twenty-six elkdogs were dangerous to get on. The other twenty-one were easier to ride but not always perfect. Each rider knew he had to be ready for anything as he rode one of these animals.

Day after day the men rode. From dawn to dark, the elkdogs were ridden. Soon the men noticed that the elkdogs did not run as they did at first. They would rather stand still than move at all. They became hard to handle. The men were using the elkdogs so much that they were not getting enough food or rest.

Some of the older men who knew dogs well were the first to say that the men were working the animals too hard and not giving them time to eat and rest. It was decided to allow the elkdogs time each day to graze on the rich grass near the river. Guards would watch them day and night. They would be tied to stakes at night. In the morning they were led to the corral so the men could have their turns riding them.

The next step was to take elkdogs out on a hunt. The two men who had seen the enemy hunters ride elkdogs next to the mighty buffalo told their hunters exactly how it was done. Immediately many young warriors asked to be the first to try a hunt on elkdogs. They bragged about their bravery and their skill at riding the speedy elkdogs.

In the end the five warriors who had captured this first herd of elkdogs were chosen to be the first hunters to ride them. They were not very good at first. Only two riders even got close to a buffalo. The other three elkdogs were too frightened by the stampeding buffalo. They ran out of control far from the herd.

The Blackfeet hunters soon learned that only certain elkdogs were good for hunting the buffalo. They would also learn that even the best elkdogs had to be trained to run inches away from the dangerous buffalo with their sharp horns and tremendous strength. Both elkdogs and riders were in danger of instant death from the ferocious beasts.

It was Runs-Like-Antelope who was first to bring down a nice cow buffalo. The elkdog he rode was the finest of the entire herd. It was the one that the twins had captured. This elkdog had been trained to hunt buffalo by the enemy. It ran stride for stride next to a stampeding buffalo. This elkdog even seemed to know what to do to make it easy for its rider to deliver the fatal spear into the huge beast.

That same summer more raids were planned and carried out. Not all were successful. One raid resulted in the capture of no elkdogs and the loss of two brave Blackfeet warriors. Neither of these men were from Om's village. Still there was much sadness at this loss of life.

Even worse, the men's bodies fell into enemy hands. No burial was possible. The mourning went on for days. Woman cried and wailed loudly and many cut their hair short. Long hair was a symbol of a good soul full of love, joy, and pride. To cut your hair short was to show great respect and love for the person who died.

Om saw so many changes in his life that summer. It seemed hard for him to realize what it all meant to him and his future. Truly the elkdog was one of the greatest things that could ever have happened in a Blackfeet Indian boy's lifetime. And this was just the beginning of Om's adventures with the amazing elkdog.

10

Powerful Medicine

By the end of summer the Blackfeet warriors had captured sixty-one elkdogs from their enemies. Another herd of about thirty animals was captured but lost when a large party of enemy warriors caught up with the Blackfeet raiders and took the elkdogs back. The Blackfeet braves were lucky to escape with their lives.

When Om's people broke summer camp for their journey south, eight of the sixty-one horses belonged to his band. They used four as pack animals. The other four were ridden by scouts who could now go farther and faster than they ever could on foot.

Om and Twin Girl were allowed to lead the elkdogs that carried packs. This was a great honor which filled the twins with pride. Om even taught Wise Bird to ride on the elkdog's pack.

Each time the people camped everyone wanted to ride an elkdog. First the leaders made sure each animal was well fed and watered. Special campsites were picked where there was plenty of good grass for the eight elkdogs. The people talked about how easy it was to feed the elkdogs. They didn't eat meat like dogs did. All elkdogs needed was grass and water. This truly amazed the people. Elkdogs were wonderful animals.

Om had ridden elkdogs a few times that summer. Since he was only a boy, his rides were short. It made him even more eager to ride longer and farther. He longed for the day he would have his own elkdog to ride far from the camp on a hunt or to scout for the enemy. He knew he had a long time to wait for this to happen. He kept this dream in his heart and knew it would come true someday.

The trip to winter camp took many weeks, but time went fast for Om. The route was familiar, as the people returned to the same camp they used the winter before. This winter the people would know the valley better. The hunters had learned the best places to hunt. The hot spring Om discovered the year before would be used and enjoyed by all the people.

The men had talked about where they could find grass for the elkdogs during the winter. They knew the snows would cover much of the grass. Just above their camp the slopes were windblown and some grass would be easy for elkdogs to get. The men decided there was enough grass there to keep the eight elkdogs healthy for the winter.

Om was excited the day the people reached their winter camp. Many of their lodgepoles were still standing against the trees where the people had stored them last spring.

It was still fall-like weather. Days were warm. Nights were cold and frosty. Each day Om still wore only his breechcloth and went barefoot. His first trip to the hot spring caused him to remember his overnight stay there the past winter. It seemed that it had happened only a short time ago.

Om loved to explore new places. His discovery of the bull elk, the hot spring, and his capture of the elkdog made him hungry for more excitement and discoveries. Whenever the boy had a chance, he loved to go off on his own to explore new places. His father told him he could never leave without first asking if he was needed for any work in the camp. Om was always obedient and asked permission to leave the village. Wise Bird always went with him on his trips away from the camp.

On a bright clear day Om had permission to leave for the day. The night before he had gathered everything he needed for his day of exploration. At dawn the boy was up and on his way. He wore a winter suit and warm moccasins. If the day became warm, he would take his winter suit off and wear only his breechcloth.

Om was excited to have a day of his own. This hadn't happened for a long time.

Instead of heading for the hot spring, Om went straight west toward the big river. He was so excited about having a whole day to go exploring that he broke into a run. He made up his mind to see more of the river and the valley than he had had a chance to see his first winter in this valley.

Om was good at picking an easy route to follow. He stayed away from creek bottoms where willow bushes and cottonwood trees were thick. The open slopes were the best. Still the boy had to watch his step, or he could put his foot into a badger's hole and break his leg.

Om's energy seemed endless. He was feeling great. He was smart enough to pace himself so he would not tire himself too soon. The boy slowed down and walked after each long run. He stopped to look in every direction for animals or even the enemy. He couldn't look around much while he was running over the uneven ground. His stops were good times to catch his breath while he looked around. Each rest stop was made on a high spot where Om had a good view of all the land around him.

Om was close to the big river before he knew it. He saw Wise Bird land on the rocks next to the water. The raven dipped his beak in many times to drink his fill of the cool water. Then the boy's eyes went from Wise Bird to the sky high above. There he saw a huge bald eagle

gliding above the river. The boy knew the eagle was fish-
ing. He watched the great bird's head turn from side to
side as it searched for trout.

Just before Om started to move on, he saw the majestic eagle swoop toward the river. When the huge bird
reached the surface, it dropped its talons into the water.
The razor-sharp claws clamped onto a two-pound trout.
Instantly the eagle pulled the fish into the air and with its
powerful wings began to climb higher and higher.

It was a wonderful thing to see. Om knew the eagle
was a great bird. His people treasured eagle feathers and
gave them to warriors who did great things. The boy
hoped to have a big headdress full of eagle feathers he
earned for brave things he would do in his lifetime.

As Om watched the eagle circle over the river, his
eyes saw something fall from the beautiful bird. It was
one of his tail feathers. The boy couldn't believe his
eyes. There right before his eyes an eagle feather was
floating to the ground. Om stood absolutely still. He
kept his eyes fastened on the beautiful feather as it
drifted downward. The boy didn't dare move. He might

lose sight of this treasure. He had to have it. He must not lose it.

The feather just missed landing in a cottonwood tree. It slipped through the branches and landed on a pile of brush. It was just across the river.

Keeping his eye on the big tree, Om ran upstream to a safe place to cross the river. There was a strong current, but the water was shallow. He was careful not to slip on the rounded rocks.

Om reached the other side and dashed to the brush pile under the big tree. There it was right on top of the pile, a perfect eagle feather. The excited boy carefully picked it from its resting place. He stood for several minutes looking at its great beauty.

This was a special gift, a special prize, and a sign of good fortune for the finder. Om was holding a treasure right in his hand. This was a great day.

Holding the feather tightly, Om ran up the hillside away from the river. He looked up at the sun. The day was not even half over. Should he hurry back to camp to show his feather to everyone? Should he explore some more?

The boy stood thinking for a few minutes. Then he said out loud, "The day is still new. Maybe I will not have another day like this for a long time. I will go on to look for more treasures."

Om moved away from the river and worked his way upstream and farther south. This land was all new to him. His plan was to go farther up river, cross at a new place, and head back to his village a whole new way.

As the boy climbed a ridge for a better view of his route south, he had a strange feeling he was being watched or that something was about to happen to him. The feeling was so strong that Om dashed to a large tree to get out of sight.

Wise Bird was nowhere in sight. There were no sounds. A slight breeze came across the ridge. There was nothing unusual anywhere near Om. Still he knew something had changed. He was glad he had his bow and arrows and knife, but what was it that gave him such a strange feeling?

Suddenly Om knew what it was. It was a smell. Yes, a smell he knew. The smell meant elkdogs were near. Carefully the boy moved away from the tree in the direction of the breeze. He had walked only a short distance when he came to a sudden stop. There at his feet were fresh droppings left by an elkdog. Where were the elkdogs? Was the enemy near? What should he do?

Om ran a little farther, following tracks left by elkdogs. Now he came to many more tracks and droppings. At least twenty elkdogs had gone by this place that morning. Where were they now? How many enemy warriors were with them?

The boy hoped he could see the enemy, cross the river, and get back to his village and warn his people. He wouldn't look very far before he started back. He stayed hidden as he made his plan.

I'll stay in the bushes and trees, climb one more hill, and look for the enemy. Then I'll run faster than I ever have before to warn my people, Om decided.

Om started on his climb up the hill, staying mostly in the trees and bushes. When he came to an open place, he crossed it at top speed. He crouched down while he caught his breath. He looked around and right in front of him saw a gully filled with trees and bushes. It led straight up the hill. Om decided he could climb up the ravine and not be seen. When he got high enough, he could go out to a place for a good view of all the lands around him. This would give him a chance to see the enemy without being seen himself.

Om ran for the gully and hurried uphill through bushes, over fallen trees, between large rocks, until he was out of breath. Now he would take a look. The top of the hill was only a short walk away.

The boy turned left and climbed out of the gully to the open hilltop. As he walked, his eyes scanned the view in every direction. All was well until Om came to the highest point on the hill. He was not far from a large rock when he saw a sight that terrified him. There sitting on an elkdog only one hundred feet away was an enemy warrior. He was coming uphill and was riding a gray elkdog.

Om froze in his tracks. One idea filled his mind: Run! He turned to dash back into the gully. It was his only chance. He could run through the bushes, rocks, and fallen trees. Elkdogs could never follow him down the gully. Om spun around, ran ten steps, and saw another enemy warrior. This one was blocking his way to the gully. This enemy also sat on an elkdog. The boy turned once more. This time he would head straight downhill in the open in a try to escape. One look in that direction, and Om knew he was caught. There were enemy warriors all around him, six of them. They just sat on their elkdogs, staring at this lone boy.

All Om could think about was what would happen to him now. Would the enemy kill him? Would they torture him? Would he become a slave? What about his people, his mother, his father, his sisters, his friends? Would he ever see them again? And what about Wise Bird?

It seemed that this terrible moment would ruin his whole life. Om had a hollow, sick feeling in his stomach. This day of great happiness had turned into a day of horror.

The boy knew what he must do to avoid instant death. He took his bow and arrows and knife and laid them on the ground. He stepped back several feet and bowed his head. This was a sign of surrender.

The enemy warriors watched from a distance. They had hoped the boy would run from them and lead them to his people. That was the last thing the boy would ever do. Om would die before he would lead the enemy to his people.

One warrior gave a signal and all six men rode their elkdogs slowly toward the boy. They were only fifty feet from Om when suddenly they all stopped. Their heads were turned to see a huge raven dive from high in the bright blue sky straight toward the boy.

Just above Om's head the raven pulled out of its steep dive and began circling over the enemy warriors' heads. The raven was squawking louder than these men had ever heard a raven squawk.

The boy couldn't believe his eyes. It was Wise Bird. He had been following Om all along. What is Wise Bird trying to do? Does he think he can drive the enemy away? Like the enemy warriors, the boy stood there in great wonder at the raven's actions.

Wise Bird flapped his powerful wings against the calm air. The great raven looked larger than ever to Om. Several times he circled close to the heads of the six men. Their elkdogs were frightened and reared up and pranced while the warriors hung on tightly.

After Wise Bird's last trip over the enemy, the spectacular bird flew to Om. He landed on the boy's shoulder,
tucked his wings, and put his beak next to Om's face.

The enemy was frightened by the low-flying, strange-
acting bird. Now they were dumbfounded. They could
not believe their eyes. What strange power does this boy
have that he can call a raven from the sky? Is this boy
from the spirit world? They could only sit and stare and
wonder about this strange sight.

Om saw the looks on the warriors' faces. He knew
they were amazed by Wise Bird. Maybe they were afraid
of something they could not understand. The boy knew
he had a chance. He would show these warriors some
more big medicine. Om held out his right arm and
tapped it with his left hand. Immediately Wise Bird
jumped onto the arm. The boy reached into the hide bag
tied to his waist. He pulled out a piece of dried buffalo
meat and fed it to the raven. Wise Bird swallowed it in
one gulp.

Next Om bent down and picked up a small stick. He
threw it fifteen feet in front of him. With a wave of Om's
left hand, Wise Bird took to the air and flew right to the

stick. With his large beak, the raven picked up the stick and flew back to the boy's shoulder. The big bird put the stick in Om's hand and let out three loud squawks.

Now the boy would have Wise Bird do his newest trick. If the raven could do this one, Om knew the enemy would be even more amazed. The boy made a sweeping motion with his arm which signaled Wise Bird to fly. The raven took off flying in a wide circle around Om. At exactly the right time the boy tossed the stick high into the air. In a flash Wise Bird swooped under the stick, did a complete rollover, and clamped his beak on the stick in midair.

Wise Bird made one more circle with the stick held tightly in his beak. The raven came in and landed on Om's head. The boy put his hands up by his forehead and Wise Bird dropped the stick into his hands.

Om had not noticed, but the men behind him had started riding their elkdogs around him to get to their friends. In minutes all the enemy warriors were together. They talked quietly as they kept watching this amazing boy and the raven that obeyed him.

The six warriors were afraid of the powerful medicine this strange boy possessed. They were sure he was from the spirit world. Anything they could not explain frightened them greatly. To hurt this boy or take him prisoner might make the spirits angry. It could cause many bad things to happen or even cause their deaths.

As the men spoke, Om bent over forward with his arms extended out from his sides. Wise Bird began walking from one hand, down his arm, across his shoulders and neck, and over his arm to his other hand. All the time the raven squawked loudly. It was a strange scene indeed.

The six warriors turned their elkdogs and galloped away. They were happy to leave without any terrible thing happening to them.

Om stood there trying his best to understand all that had just happened to him. He didn't know whether to feel happy or afraid. He did look at his hands, which were trembling. He noticed a dizzy feeling come over him. He had just gone through an event that would terrify any grown man.

11

In the Lair of the Enemy

Om didn't stand still for long. He knew the enemy was afraid of his special powers with the raven, but how long would they stay afraid? They might think it over and come back after him.

The boy signaled the amazing Wise Bird to follow him. Off he ran to the gully and down the creekbed. He stepped only on rocks so he would leave no tracks.

When Om decided to leave the bush-filled gully, he knew he would have to cover his trail the best he could. If he left tracks on the ground the enemy would find him easily. The boy tried to think about everything he needed to do to make his escape. One mistake and he could be caught.

The boy looked at the open hillside he would have to cross to get to the next creekbed. Om moved over to a spruce tree, grabbed one of its lower branches, and pulled with all his strength until it snapped off. Then he started backward across the open hillside. He bent over, using the long spruce branch like a broom. He brushed it gently over the track he was leaving. The needles erased his footprints as he moved backward as fast as possible.

In minutes Om was across the hillside and dropping into the next creekbed. This one had water running through it. There was not much water, but it would be helpful. First, he needed a drink. Second, he could walk in the shallow water and leave no tracks at all.

Down the creekbed Om traveled, stopping often to look and listen for danger. He felt like a hunted animal. He felt lonely. At each stop the boy hid in the thick bushes or between several spruce trees. He knew he couldn't go back to his village until he was sure he

wasn't being followed. Om was ready to die before he would lead the enemy to his people.

The boy had not eaten since morning. The afternoon was half gone as Om found some thick bushes to push his way into so he could hide and enjoy some food. These bushes were on the edge of the creekbed, and Om could look out at a large open field to his right.

The hungry boy was finishing his last few bites of dried meat when he heard hoofbeats coming his way. Elkdogs! Running! They're coming right at me! he thought.

It was several minutes before Om saw the first elk-dogs. They galloped across the open area right next to the boy. Om crouched even lower in the bushes while he still kept his eyes on this scene. The first elkdog was black with a white diamond on its face. The beautiful animal held its head high and its long tail and mane were blown back as it raced in front of the herd. Right behind came four enemy riders herding at least twenty elkdogs. They didn't know Om was hiding just a few feet away from the nearest rider.

The boy didn't move a muscle. He hardly even took a breath. He was close to death or capture for the second time that day. Om studied the enemy riders. He recognized two of them. They had been among the men who had surrounded him on the hilltop less than two hours ago.

Now Om could put the puzzle together. The tracks he had seen earlier were made by these men and elkdogs. When he went up the gully, Om had walked right into the enemy path. They left their herd to capture him. When Wise Bird frightened them away, they returned to their herd of elkdogs and were moving south again.

The boy watched as the last rider disappeared over the crest of the hill. Om would stay hidden until he was sure it was safe to leave. He felt even more alone now. The more he thought about all that had happened, the more he shuddered to think about what could have happened to him. The amazing Wise Bird saved my life. He found the elk when our people were hungry. He found the lost baby. Om knew his wonderful raven was truly a great gift from the Above One.

Where was Wise Bird now? Om knew the day would end soon. The sun was crossing the sky toward the western mountains. The boy would leave his hiding place soon and head back to his village. He didn't know it, but his raven was resting far above him in a spruce tree. It seemed that Wise Bird knew his master was hiding from the men. It also looked like the raven was too smart to go near Om while the enemy was nearby. Wise Bird would never lead the enemy to his master.

When Om was quite sure the enemy was far enough away, he started wading the creek down toward the great river. He wanted to cross the river safely while there was still daylight. Then he would stay away from the patchy snowfields, travel fast, and not leave any easy-to-see tracks. As Om traveled he thought about all that had happened. In all his thoughts he kept seeing the beautiful black elkdog with the white diamond marking its face. He could not stop thinking about this spectacular animal. He had never seen such a beautiful creature. It was as black as Wise Bird. It held its head so high. Its eyes sparkled in the sunlight.

Om had seen this great elkdog only for thirty seconds. In that short time the boy had noticed all these details. It was almost as if he had seen this beautiful animal many times before. Om had a strong feeling that he would see the big black elkdog again. He even tingled with the excitement of a dream that someday he would ride this elkdog across the very ground he now walked.

The sun was dipping below the western mountains as Om walked out of the shallow water on the east side of the great river. A large tree that had fallen from the west bank lay across the deepest pool of water. It helped Om make a quick, safe crossing.

Now the long run began. With Wise Bird far ahead, Om ran hard over the land, racing the coming darkness. Om wanted to be on familiar ground before it became pitch dark.

Wise Bird had flown nonstop back to the village. Twin Girl saw him first. The raven had made it right at dark. The big bird landed at the girl's feet.

"Wise Bird! You are here," said Twin Girl. "Om-kas-toe must be close to the village. Where have you been? I have had to do all the work. You have been no help. Your trip must have been a long one. Did you get lost?" The girl talked to the raven as though he were Om. She was glad to see him.

Only Om's mother, Tall Woman, had worried about him. Everyone else was too busy getting ready to eat and to sit by their warm fires to talk before rolling up in their warm buffalo furs to sleep. The people knew that often Om went off on his own, and hadn't he come back late before?

The boy was finally coming to the hot spring as total darkness settled over the land. He still had a long run ahead of him. He was so weary his legs felt like logs. His throat was dry. His arms were heavy. He ached all over. He was bone weary but somehow he must run on with his news of the enemy.

The smell of hot water drew Om toward the spring. He decided he would rest there. The hot water would be good for his exhausted body.

As Om came up the rise to the hot spring, he stopped. He heard voices. They were familiar voices. The boy rushed through the darkness toward a campfire just ahead. The men around the fire jumped to their feet. Two of them grabbed their spears.

"I am Om-kas-toe. I have returned! I have seen the enemy!"

These were all the words the boy could blurt out. He was gasping for each breath. In the firelight Om saw the faces of these five men. They were all from his village. White Wolf was the first to speak.

"Om-kas-toe! What is your message? Where is the enemy? How many warriors are there? How is it that you found them?"

Before the boy could speak a sixth man walked into the firelight. It was Om's father, Otterman.

"My son, come to the fire, sit, let your breath return to you. Drink this water. When you are ready, speak, my son. Tell us the message you have."

While Om drank and rested, the men told him they were at the hot spring to build a small dome of hide over the hot water. This would make a wonderful sweathut for the people. They told the boy he could soothe his body in the water and in the hut when he finished his story.

As Om spoke, the men listened in complete silence. Did he truly see the enemy? Did the raven really save him from six enemy warriors? Was there really an elkdog the color the boy described? When Om told about the gully, the hilltop, the creekbeds, all in such detail, the men were sure it had not been a dream.

After Om finished his story, the men asked him many questions. How long did it take him to get to the place where he first saw the enemy tracks? How many men did he see? What weapons did they carry? From the boy's accurate description the men knew just about all they needed to know.

"You have done well, my son," said Otterman. "We have fresh roasted deer meat for you."

The tender, juicy meat was the best Om had ever tasted. He was so glad his run was finished. Now the boy wondered how he ever could have kept going the rest of the way to the village that night.

The hot water was even better than the delicious meat. Om lowered himself into the pool slowly. Right away the hot water began to work its magic on the boy's muscles. Several times Om dipped his head under. Many

of his aches and pains melted away. This was a wonderful ending to the scariest day of Om's life.

The hot water made Om feel a little dizzy after a
while. His people had learned it was not good to stay in
the hot water too long. The boy slowly pulled himself
out into the refreshing cold air. When he was dry, he was
given a warm robe. The next morning he would try the
sweathut.

The men had put up a tepee a short distance from the
pool. They all crowded into it for a good night's sleep.
While Om soaked in the water, the men had planned
what to do the next day. They would be up very early.
With the enemy in their valley, the Blackfeet would have
to move fast to protect their people. No time could be
wasted.

The weary boy slept poorly that night. He rolled and
tossed. He dreamed strange dreams. He saw the big
black elkdog run past him over and over again.

The night seemed very short. The men were up
before daylight. Om heard them talking quietly around
the morning fire. The plan was to send three men back
to the village to warn the people and to wait for a mes-

sage telling them what to do next. The other three men would follow Om-kas-toe back to the place where he saw the enemy. This would be another day of great adventure for the boy who had already had more excitement in his life than all the boys his age put together.

12

An Important Message

Om rubbed his eyes as he sat up in the buffalo robe. He walked stiffly to the campfire just outside the tepee. He was given some more deer meat as he sat listening to his father tell about their plans.

"Om-kas-toe, you will lead us to the enemy trail. We will follow their tracks. We will find their camp. While two of us watch the enemy, the other two will return to our village with a report. We must find the enemy, know how many warriors they have, and where they are going.

When we learn these things, we will know what we must do to protect our families."

Otterman's words made Om's heart beat fast. He had an important job. He must not fail. Could he find the way to the enemy trail? What would happen when they did find the tracks? How much farther had the enemy gone? If they found the Snake warriors, what would happen then? For a young boy, these were exciting questions.

The sky was showing the first signs of dawn when Om was finishing his deer meat. The three men who were going back to the village had already left. The boy hardly noticed the cold. He was so excited, it was hard to think about anything but the job ahead of him.

When all was ready, the fire was put out. The men checked their weapons, and Otterman signaled Om to lead the way. The boy headed straight west in a direct line to the great river. It was easy to find his crossing place. He just ran upstream until he saw the large tree laying across the deep part of the river.

After leading the three men across, Om headed out of the river bottom up to higher ground. The sun was up now as the boy ran to the base of the hills west of the great river. He was relieved when he saw the familiar creek flowing down out of the gully.

The boy led the men into the trees and bushes to keep out of sight of the enemy. To succeed, the Blackfeet would have to see the enemy before the enemy saw them. Once again Om was hiding. This time he was not alone. What a difference it was to have his father and two other warriors with him. He felt so much safer than he did when he had traveled this creekbed alone.

The boy climbed the creekbed for a long time. He thought it seemed farther than it should. He began to worry that he had gone too far. His worry ended when he came to the exact place where he had crouched in the bushes, watching the enemy go by with their herd of elkdogs.

This is where Om's guiding work ended. Otterman and the two men quietly made their plan. One man would go out onto the hillside to check the trail. He would return with his report so the men could decide what to do next.

The man returned with a good report. He found the trail. It would be easy to follow and still stay hidden most of the time. The enemy was driving the elkdogs across the sides of the hills to avoid the valley floor below. Maybe this was just a small number of the enemy. Maybe the Blackfeet warriors outnumbered the enemy. This would mean they could make a surprise attack and capture all the elkdogs.

With the plan made, the run began. Running on the sides of hills was hard and tiring. Staying close to trees and bushes made it even harder. The pace was steady and few stops were made. Not a word was spoken. Hand signals were used. Om knew he had done his job. He hoped to get another chance to help. He knew the men were grateful that he had found the enemy, made his miraculous escape, and came back to lead them to this trail so quickly.

Om's muscles loosened again. He had no trouble keeping up. The run was over all new ground. The boy was getting a chance to see even more new places. The four runners crossed one hillside after another. They passed through several gullies and creeks. They ran until suddenly the trail turned sharply to the right and up an open slope.

Now the four had to be more careful. There were fewer trees and bushes to hide them from view. A stop was made to talk things over. The men noticed that the elkdogs had walked up this slope quite slowly. The tracks told that story. It was decided it would be best to leave the trail and do what Om had done. They would make their climb in a gully next to the open slope. They hadn't gone far when Otterman raised his hand to signal a stop. The gully opened into a saddle between two hills. The saddle was the beginning of a large meadow with a small pond and a tiny creek.

Otterman motioned the rest to stay hidden while he went into the meadow for a look. He was gone only a few minutes. He came back to say that the enemy had camped in this meadow the night before. Fresh tracks left the meadow on the other side and headed south again.

The men decided that now two of them should return to their village for help. They could all meet in this meadow later in the day or the next morning. White Wolf and Two Bears started their long run. Otterman and Om left to follow the enemy trail. They would meet Two

Bears and White Wolf at the meadow when they
returned with help. Otterman wanted to find the enemy
first. It would be a dangerous mission.

Om knew his father would be counting on him to
think carefully. He could be a big help. He must not do
anything that could result in a disaster for him and his
father.

"My son, we must follow the enemy. We must find
them. We must not be seen or heard. Watch my signals.
Be ready to move quickly. Run with feet of silence. Use
your eyes and ears well. We must do our work with all
our skill."

Om listened as he never had done before. His eyes
were fastened on his father's face as Otterman spoke.
The boy never saw his father look more serious. He
never heard him speak more important words. Om
knew he was needed to do his part to help protect all
the people.

The boy followed his father closely on the run across
the meadow. There were elkdog droppings everywhere.
The enemy had camped on the opposite side of the
meadow. From there the tracks went up and over a tree-

covered rise. At the top the trail left the trees and went down a gradual slope to the lower hills.

Otterman stood next to the last tree to have a look. The grass on the open slope had been trampled by the herd of elkdogs. He could see the trail go into the trees far below. Otterman decided they could circle to the left and stay hidden in the bushes and rocks as they followed the trail from a short distance away.

Once father and son reached the trees below, they saw that the trail continued straight down toward the great river. Now Otterman knew the enemy plan. Now he knew why Om was found by the Snake warriors. He signaled for a stop in a thick clump of spruce trees.

"The enemy took their elkdogs to the high meadow to camp. On the way to this hiding place, they found you, my son. You were right in their path to the meadow. Here the enemy returns to the valley to continue their journey."

Om's father was wise. He knew the enemy's plan in just this short time. The boy knew his father had learned much during his many days as a hunter and warrior. Otterman had learned the ways of men and animals. The last two days had been days of much learning for Om, also.

"Om, we will cut straight down to the great river. There you will leave me and run as fast as you can toward our village. Stay in the open so our warriors can see you. When you find them, tell them not to go up to the meadow. Tell them to follow the great river. It will save them much time. If you don't find them, go all the way to our village and wait for our return."

These words bothered Om. Return to the village. Wait. This cannot be. The boy did not want this to happen. He had a sick feeling inside, but he knew he must obey no matter how he felt. I must find our warriors. I do not want to return to our village. I must help find the enemy. I must save our warriors' time. I must see the big black elkdog again.

The black elkdog? The thought came to the boy out of nowhere. The black elkdog was his main reason for wanting to go on with the warriors. The boy even thought that the big black elkdog was waiting for him. It was a strange idea indeed.

When Om left his father near the great river, he looked once more at the marker they would use to know this exact place of parting. It would be easy to find again. The marker was a huge pine tree that stood by itself. There was no other tree like it anywhere along the river.

Om started running north with one thought in mind. He had to find and meet Two Bears, White Wolf, and the rest of the warriors. If he didn't he would have to keep going all the way to the village. This would end his great adventure. The boy knew that the faster he ran the better his chances were. He ran faster than he ever had in his life. After he fell and skinned a knee, he slowed down a little.

As Om ran, he thought of an idea that might work. He didn't want to run too far downriver. He might miss the place where the warriors would cross the river. He would stop here where he could see much of the river. He would think about distances and time. He could figure out about where the warriors were if his ideas were accurate.

Om started from the beginning. He thought about each part of his trip since he had left the village the morning before. He thought about the time it took him to get to each place. Then he thought about the high meadow that Two Bears and White Wolf had left to return to camp. He tried to estimate as closely as possible just where the men might be at this moment.

Om became worried. Maybe he had run too far. The boy's thoughts were suddenly interrupted by the sound of Wise Bird's flapping wings. The graceful raven glided to the ground and landed at Om's feet. The boy was happy to see his pet raven and pulled out a piece of deer meat for him. Om's mind was not on Wise Bird. He was still thinking about having to find the warriors. They must be close to this place, Om said to himself. I'll climb higher where I can see even more. This will give me the best chance of seeing our warriors.

When Om stood up, Wise Bird took to the air, flying high above the boy. Oh, Wise Bird, if only I could send you off to find our warriors. You can see so much and fly so high and fast. If only I, too, could fly as you do. I could find our men.

No sooner had Om thought these thoughts than he heard a call. It sounded like someone calling his name. It

must be Wise Bird. He makes strange sounds, Om thought. Then the sound came again. This time it was a little louder. Someone was calling his name! Om ran to a place where he could look downhill better. As he got to the best spot, the boy saw eight warriors run out of the trees and into the open. It was his people. Om had stopped at exactly the right time and in just the right place.

The men dashed up hill to Om. The boy was so excited and relieved to see them that he almost forgot the important message he had for them.

"Om-kas-toe, it is you. We saw the great raven flying above this hill. His flight led us to you," said White Wolf.

Wise Bird had found the men. Had the warriors not seen the high-flying raven, they would have gone right past Om. Now the boy could give them his father's important message.

"White Wolf, we have found the enemy's trail in the valley. You must not go to the high meadow. Stay in the valley along the great river. My father sends you this message to save your feet much time. The enemy is near with many elkdogs. Otterman sent me to lead you."

Without another word, White Wolf waved to Om to run on. The eight warriors followed him closely.

Om's words went through his mind over and over. "The enemy is near. Many elkdogs. Stay in the valley. My father sent me."

Also in the boy's mind was the vision of the big black elkdog. Somehow Om could not stop thinking about the beautiful animal. Somehow he knew his return to his father and the search for the enemy would lead him to the great elkdog. He had the strange but very real feeling that every stride he was taking as he led the men was leading him to the majestic black elkdog.

13

Beautiful Black Elkdog

Om retraced his steps to the tall pine tree near the river. Here the men picked up Otterman's trail leading south. The run continued for several hours. Om began to feel tired. He had covered many miles the last two days. No matter how weary he felt, he would never let the warriors know it. He ran on without a complaint. He still had his job to do. He still had his dream of seeing the black elkdog again.

Om forced himself to keep going. Would the men ever stop for a rest? Would they ever find his father? I must keep going no matter what. The boy wasn't expecting such a sudden stop. Two Bears stopped so fast that White Wolf nearly knocked him over from behind.

Two Bears dropped to his knees. He crouched behind a pile of broken rock. He peered over the pile at the scene ahead. There next to a creek grazed about twenty elkdogs. A few were drinking from the stream. Enemy warriors rested in the grass near some trees. They had no idea the Blackfeet were watching them. They were careless. They had no guards posted. Om was grateful for the rest. He was beginning to catch his breath when he saw a movement off to his left. It was someone crawling through the brush toward them. Quickly Om tapped the man in front of him and pointed at the approaching figure. The men got their weapons ready for a fight.

In a few seconds the person could be seen much better. It was Otterman! All were relieved to see him, especially Om. Minutes later Otterman arrived at the hiding place.

"Snake warriors. Seven of them. Twenty-one elkdogs. We can follow. At a good time and place we will attack and take their elkdogs," whispered Otterman.

"The enemy are fools. They have no guards, no scouts. The attack will be easy," whispered Two Bears.

"Let us attack now," said White Wolf.

"This is not a good place," Otterman said quietly. "The land is too rough. Too much rock. Too many fallen trees. Our escape would be slow. We must follow the enemy to a better place. Then we will attack, take the elkdogs, and make our escape."

The men listened to Otterman's words. They decided he spoke with wisdom. He had been at this place longer. He had had time to think and plan.

The Blackfeet followed the enemy for the rest of the afternoon. Their pace was slow. Om was glad. He was still tired. He did get one glimpse of the big black elkdog on the way, but it was from a great distance.

When the Snake warriors made camp, the nine Blackfeet men and Om found a good hiding place in a dense stand of fir trees. The men would take turns watching the enemy camp all night. When the sky showed the very first signs of dawn, the men would inch their way to the enemy camp on their stomachs. The attack would be a complete surprise. The Blackfeet could escape on the elkdogs while they took the whole herd with them. They would take several days to return to their village to make sure they weren't being followed.

Om was extremely tired. Darkness came, and the air became cold. The boy's muscles stiffened. He did not sleep much. There were no blankets. Om was uncomfortable all night. His mind wandered as he thought about all that had happened. It all seemed so mixed up. It was hard to think about what might happen the next day. The boy felt so miserable that he wasn't even nervous about what lay ahead of him.

Once during the night Otterman spoke softly to his son. "Om-kas-toe, before we attack the enemy, you must move down closer to the great river. After our attack, we will drive the elkdogs toward you. Have a rope ready. Let the elkdogs see you. Stand still. We will want them to stop. Catch one. We will catch ours. All of us will ride away and drive the rest of the elkdogs before us."

Even these words did not excite Om. He was so tired, so stiff, so cold. The boy didn't feel like ever moving from this place. He wanted only to find a warm bed and sleep. Om knew he had to stop thinking this way.

No matter what, he would do what his father asked him to do.

After his father spoke to him, the weary boy fell into a deep sleep. He rolled over and over as he dreamed. In his dream he saw the big black elkdog running at top speed. There was a rider on its back. It was Twin Girl. A dog ran beside elkdog. It was Thunder. Then Wise Bird flew into Om's dream. The girl, the dog, the raven, and the elkdog all seemed to be looking for something. What was it that they were searching everywhere for? Why was Twin Girl riding the black elkdog? Suddenly Om's dream was interrupted.

"Quiet! You dream, my son. You speak out loud in your sleep. Sleep is over. We prepare for the attack. Eat this meat. Drink much water. Your strength will return. Your body will become warm again."

The groggy boy stood stretching his arms and legs. He ate and drank as he moved about. As his father said, Om did feel better. Minutes later he was moving silently through the trees in the early morning darkness. With each step, he began to realize the great danger that surrounded him. His father and the other warriors at this very minute were crawling toward the sleeping enemy. Soon they would attack. Again Om was alone, but he would be ready.

The boy picked a perfect hiding place where he could easily see the open area that the elkdogs would enter on their run downhill. Om waited and waited. The attack did not come. The boy strained to hear even the faintest sound. The daylight became brighter and brighter. Om knew something was seriously wrong. What could it be? Where were the Blackfeet warriors? Would his father come for him? What should he do? Om did not have to decide. Everything changed before he had time to think. Out into the open walked the herd of elkdogs. There in front stood the big black one. The animals were not running. They were not frightened. They had not been chased. The elkdogs just grazed lazily on the deep grass. The boy did not know what this meant. He just watched and wondered.

Strangely, the black elkdog did not graze. It just kept moving toward Om's hiding place. The closer the big animal came, the more excited the boy got. It's coming right to me, thought Om. It knows I'm here. I will go to the beautiful elkdog.

Slowly the boy stood up and very slowly he walked into the open. This caused the big black animal to stop. Its ears were cocked forward to pick up any sound the boy made. Its nostrils opened and closed rapidly as the animal sniffed the air.

For a few seconds both boy and elkdog stood motionless, looking at each other. When Om began moving again, the black elkdog did not move at all. The other animals stopped grazing to look at the boy. Then one by one they started grazing again.

The boy continued to walk very slowly toward the elkdog. He held a rope with a loop tied at the end. He had a feeling that all this was part of a strange dream. Om felt this had all happened to him before just this way. As if in a trance, the boy walked right up to the beautiful black elkdog. The animal never moved.

Carefully Om reached out and rubbed the great animal's neck. The elkdog threw its head back twice, then nudged the boy's shoulder with it nose. Om could not take his eyes off the shiny black coat of this wonderful creature. He took the loop of rope in one hand and slipped it over elkdog's nose.

Just as the loop was in place, Om was startled by a shrill cry that pierced the morning air. There, only a hundred feet away, stood an enemy warrior. His cry brought more warriors to the edge of the clearing.

In a single motion, Om's feet left the ground, and he slid onto the great elkdog's back. His heels pinched the animal's sides, and the elkdog carried the boy swiftly downhill toward the great river.

As quickly as possible, the enemy warriors caught their elkdogs and rode off after the boy at full speed. Om hung onto the galloping elkdog with both hands. He had never ridden this fast. He had not had very many chances to ride elkdogs. Now he had to ride for his life. The enemy warriors had no trouble following him. The day was cloudy but bright. Om had no idea where he was going or how he could ever escape the hard-riding enemy. The boy just clung to the neck of the big black elkdog and rode on. He gave the animal its own way. He sensed that elkdog would do better picking its way.

Several times Om was able to look back over his shoulder and could see the enemy riders following. At first they didn't seem to be getting any closer. Then he saw them split up. Three stayed behind him and two cut off to the right. Om just rode on.

When the big black elkdog began turning right, Om knew the enemy's plan. They were trying to cut him off. Still the boy let elkdog run. He relied on the galloping animal to outrun the enemy. He had a good feeling that somehow the great elkdog would get him out of this trap.

Om knew the great river couldn't be too much farther. He was near the valley floor now and could see a great distance ahead. As his elkdog crossed a broad slope, the boy's heart sank. There on his right were two enemy warriors riding straight at him. They were only a hundred feet away. It looked very bad for Om. The warriors carried bows and arrows and would soon be close enough for a shot at him.

The warriors screamed their war cries. They rode at an angle to meet the boy a short distance ahead. The yells of the charging warriors seemed to cause the big

black mare to run faster and faster. Still it looked like the big elkdog was headed for a meeting with the warriors and death for Om.

The boy leaned forward even more as the first enemy arrow sailed over his back. The second arrow passed in front of elkdog's head. Om was sure an arrow would soon hit him or his elkdog. He thought about surrender, but there was no way he could stop this great animal. He would just have to ride to his death.

The enemy did not shoot another arrow. They were waiting until their elkdogs got to the next small hilltop. A shot from there would be an easy one. They would be only forty feet from Om.

They never got a chance to pull their bow strings. They had waited just long enough for a miracle to happen. There just over the hill top the big black mare galloped into a herd of grazing buffalo. The big animal never panicked. She ran straight into the center of the herd of wild beasts and out the other side. The buffalo did not bother the amazing elkdog at all.

It was a different story for the enemy warriors. The buffalo were startled and began to stampede. The warriors' elkdogs reared and twisted and turned to avoid the charging buffalo. Both riders were thrown to the ground as their animals galloped away. The other three riders stopped before they got too close. The chase was over. The miracle happened. Om escaped, riding the elkdog of his dreams.

"Thank you, Big Black," Om said over and over to the beautiful animal. "Now you have a name. You are Big Black. Thank you for saving Om-kas-toe."

The boy rode to the great river and urged Big Black across and out onto the east side. A cold rain began to fall as he came out of the riverbottom. Boy and elkdog were enveloped in a dense mist.

The rain had come at a perfect time. It would erase his tracks so the enemy could not follow. Om and the big black mare were a strange sight as they dashed through the rain and mist to safety.

Om finally realized that he had actually made his escape. He could not see or hear the enemy. Still he was filled with fear. He dared not relax. He would keep Big Black moving hour after hour.

The rain came down even harder. The day warmed. Boy and animal were soaked. Both were weary. It was late afternoon before Om finally stopped. He slid off Big Black. He held onto elkdog's neck. His legs were wobbly. He felt like he was still riding. He steadied himself against the mare's side.

Big Black stood still as Om took his first steps. Then the big mare shook her whole body and began grazing. All day the boy thought about the return to his village. He was far south. The enemy might be looking for him. He wasn't safe yet. At least he had made it this far, but what should he do now?

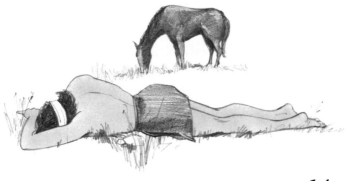

14

Near Death

The tired boy let the mare graze. He held her rope
and stood near her. Om knew the day would end soon.
He couldn't see the sun because of the clouds, but he
had ridden for many hours. His ride took him farther
and farther from home. Om would not dare start for
home for several days.

Right now the boy had to find a way to survive the
night. Om had no shelter, no buffalo robe, and very little
food. He also had to find a way to keep Big Black from
running away. Maybe he should release the mare. It

might be easier to survive and to stay hidden without the elkdog. The boy knew he owed his life to this great animal. He watched her graze so peacefully. More than anything Om wanted to keep this wonderful animal. He would not give her up until he absolutely had to do it.

Daylight began to fade. The rain had stopped. Boy and elkdog ended their rest and began the search for a place to spend the night. Om knew he could not sleep. If he fell asleep in the cold, he might never wake up. He heard his father tell about a child who was lost overnight. Even though the night was not cold enough to make ice, the child still died. Otterman told his son that cold can kill.

The boy led Big Black toward a tree-covered slope near where a small stream ran in a shallow ravine. The fir and spruce trees were thick. Om decided to hide in these trees near the creek. He would stay awake and watch the mare. When he got sleepy, he could walk her on the hillside nearby for a few minutes. It would be a long, long night.

Om led Big Black into the trees and was happy to find a small meadow, well hidden and only a short distance from the creek. Elkdog could graze there while the boy watched. The clouds would help keep the temperature from getting very low.

It was hard to stay awake. The boy's eyelids felt like heavy weights were tied to them. He dozed off many times, but never let himself go into a long sleep. Om was on his feet many times to get the stiffness out of his weary body and to help him stay awake. This was his second miserable night in a row.

The long night finally ended. The boy was very tired and sleepy. Big Black was well rested. Elkdogs can sleep standing up. Their bodies stay warm even in the coldest weather.

Om pulled himself onto the big mare's back and rode slowly away from the small meadow. He chewed on a strip of dried meat as he scanned the hills for any sign of danger. Big Black's warm body felt good on the boy's legs. It was wonderful to just sit there and let the big mare walk along.

By the middle of the morning the clouds drifted away. The warm sunshine made Om doze off right while he was riding elkdog. His head nodded when suddenly he

was awakened by the loud squawks of Wise Bird. The
boy was happy to see his friend. He thought the raven
had returned to their village.

Om stopped Big Black and slid to the ground. Wise
Bird swooped in and landed at the boy's feet. The mare
backed away and pulled at her rope.

"Do not be afraid, Big Black. Wise Bird is our friend.
Look, he comes to my arm. He eats from my hand."

The boy's words seemed to calm the nervous elkdog.
With Wise Bird sitting quietly on Om's arm the mare
became calm and began to graze, still keeping an eye on
the big raven. Big Black would soon accept the bird without fear.

The boy decided to go even farther up the great river.
He planned to cross it several times and follow a route
that the enemy could not travel easily.

Om rode the beautiful mare all that day and spent
another nearly sleepless night well hidden. He had
stopped several times to gather some roots, but other-
wise he had kept moving during the day.

On the second full day since his miraculous escape,
Om rode Big Black through a narrow part of the valley.

Large cliffs lined the west side. In the early morning he was steadily riding uphill and nearing the site of present-day Gardiner, Montana.

The boy rode over a large open area that was quite flat and then west and south up a hillside to a higher valley above the great river. Om and Big Black came out of the trees into a beautiful valley. The sun was shining brightly. It was midday. The boy became very sleepy.

Before dozing off for the third time in the last few minutes, Om smelled something familiar. It was the smell of the hot spring, but the hot spring was many miles away. Maybe he would discover a second one.

A strange feeling came over the boy. What kind of place had he wandered into? Something felt different. It was a feeling Om had never had before.

Minutes later Big Black walked through a grove of trees and into the open again. The boy and elkdog were stunned by the sight before them. There to their right was a huge ledge of bright, shiny rock. It looked like ice at first but the colors were wrong. The long ledge and cliffside were yellow, orange, and brown, and very shiny. Steam drifted into the air all around. Dead trees stood like guards here and there near the ledges. Water trick-led down in some places and ran freely in others.

Om slowly let himself slide off Big Black. He stood in complete silence. He dared not go any closer to this strange place. What does this all mean? What powerful spirits live here? Are these spirits good or evil?

What an unusual scene this was. An Indian boy, a black mare, and a tame raven standing at such an amaz-ing place. This was a place that the white man would not see for another hundred years or more. This was the place we now call Mammoth Hot Springs, which is now part of Yellowstone National Park.

Om was frightened by this strange scene. He stood absolutely still for some time before backing away slowly. His eyes would remember this sight the rest of his life. Right now he had the urge to leave this place as fast as possible. It was time to turn around and start home. This strange place made him more lonely than ever. He was ready to leave this strange place behind him.

Om headed Big Black out of this valley and back down to the great river. He was headed home. The boy

was weak from lack of food and sleep. He felt dizzy much of the time. He drank lots of water which helped keep him going. He rode leaning forward on the mare's neck. It was hard to even sit up anymore. He did manage to rise up often to look about for danger. He kept following a route that would keep him out of sight as much as possible.

The boy spent one more miserable night out. When Big Black laid down, the boy leaned against her back to keep warm and slept for about an hour. The next day Om rode on and on. By afternoon he was so weak that he didn't know where he was much of the time. He was barely able to stay on the big mare's back.

The last thing Om remembered was seeing the familiar ridges and mountains that stood above the village of his people. They seemed to be very far away. The boy did not open his eyes again. He rode on, draped forward over Big Black's shoulders and neck.

As the big mare walked on her own, the boy began to slip until he slid from Big Black. He hit the ground and lay motionless. Elkdog remained calm and began grazing near the fallen boy. Om lay in a slight depression on the open meadows leading to his village. He would not be found unless a person just happened to come this way. He was well hidden.

The boy was helpless to do anything for himself. He was unconscious. There was little more than one hour of daylight left. The temperature was falling rapidly. It would be a cold night. The boy would not survive until morning.

In Om's village most of the people believed that the boy had been captured or killed. He had been gone for too many days and nights. The boy's father and the other warriors had returned. They told their story of their try to capture the herd of elkdogs. They never made the attack. When they crawled close to the enemy camp, they counted fourteen warriors. Two of them were awake and sitting up. They could not be surprised. The Blackfeet warriors retreated to their hiding place without making an attack. Before Otterman could get to Om, the enemy saw him.

Twin Girl and Tall Woman were about the only ones in the village who believed the boy was still alive. Somehow they knew Om would return. Twin Girl was busy gathering firewood for the evening fire. Her thoughts were on her brother. Where would Om spend this cold night? Was he a prisoner? Could he ever escape? Was he still free? When would Om-kas-toe come home?

Twin Girl's thoughts went through her mind over and over. She always answered her own questions the same way. Om is alive. He will return soon. He must.

Twin Girl could not explain why, but on this particular day she was more sure than ever that Om was alive. She even had the feeling that he was close to her that very moment. She suddenly stopped her work to walk up on the hillside above their village. She looked west into the sunset. At first all Twin Girl saw was a speck of black against the bright orange sky. The girl did not move a muscle. She stood watching the speck grow larger and larger.

"Wise Bird! Wise Bird! It's you! Where is Om?"

Twin Girl ran down into the village and straight for her mother.

"Wise Bird is coming! Om is near! He is alive!"

Tall Woman scrambled out of her tepee. She stood next to Twin Girl and watched Wise Bird circle the village and come in to land on Twin Girl's arm. The raven's eyes sparkled. He cawed loudly. He jumped to the top of the girl's head and pulled at Twin Girl's hair. Then the big raven took to the air and flew in two circles above the village. With a dip and a steep banked turn, Wise Bird flew off toward the sunset.

Twin Girl never hesitated. Off she ran. Tall Woman watched as the girl ran underneath the great raven. This Indian girl's heart burned with the hope of finding her brother at the end of her run.

"Om-kas-toe! I'm coming," Twin Girl said over and over. She ran at top speed. Daylight was fading fast. Tall Woman told Otterman about the return of the raven. Tall Woman pleaded with him to go with her after Twin Girl. Otterman did not think it would do any good. The boy couldn't be near the village. It would be a waste of time. Tall Woman continued to ask him to come. When he saw the eager look on her face, he agreed to go take a look. He asked White Wolf and Two Bears to come also.

Twin Girl was already far ahead of the adults. It was getting hard for her to see Wise Bird now. Darkness was closing in fast. Twin Girl tripped and fell several times. Each time she got up and ran on just as fast as ever.

The last thing Twin Girl saw of Wise Bird was the instant he flew very low, skimming a ridge and disappearing. When the girl topped the same ridge, she could not see the raven at all. Then she heard him cawing loudly. Twin Girl ran toward the sound. She almost stumbled over Om before she saw him lying there on the cold hard ground.

The girl knelt down and gently lifted the boy's head and shoulders into her arms. He was still alive. He did not seem to be hurt except for a bruise on his forehead. Twin Girl knew Om would have died right here just a few minutes from home. The cold would have caused the boy to go to sleep forever.

When Tall Woman, Otterman, White Wolf, and Two Bears heard Twin Girl call for help, they found her with her brother. They quickly wrapped the boy in a warm buffalo robe and spoke softly about the miracle of this moment. The men lifted the boy up to carry him back to the village. As they did, Tall Woman noticed something flutter to the ground. She reached down and picked it up. It was the beautiful tail feather of an eagle. Tall Woman held the feather close to her as she followed the men to the village.

Twin Girl was at the end of the line as the men took turns carrying the unconscious boy. They had not gone too far when the girl stopped. She heard something walking behind her in the darkness. She turned to take a look. She thought she smelled an elkdog, but how could that be?

Twin Girl strained her eyes to see what was moving toward her. The first thing she saw was a white diamond and two shiny eyes. Then she saw a black elkdog walking right at her.

The girl was frightened at first, but a feeling inside her told her to stand still. When the big elkdog was just three feet from Twin Girl, it stopped. The girl saw the rope dangling to the ground. Like the time she caught the first elkdog, Twin Girl reached out and took the rope in her hand. The tired mare did not move. The surprised girl turned and led the beautiful elkdog to the village.

The excitement in the camp that night was tremendous. The boy is alive. Wise Bird has saved another life.

Twin Girl has found a big black elkdog. Tall Woman has found an eagle feather. This is a night of many wonders for this village of Blackfeet people.

The Blackfeet would not understand all that had happened until Om-kas-toe awoke and told his amazing story. Even then it would be hard for them to believe all that he told.

Om-kas-toe did tell his story. He told it so clearly that most believed. Everyone marveled at the story of Big Black, the beautiful elkdog, Om's escape through the buffalo, his visit to the land of the hot-water ledges, and his trip home.

A few people did not believe all of the boy's story. They thought some of it must be a dream. The feather is real. The big black mare is real. Maybe all his story is true. The people could only wonder at it all. Only Om-kas-toe really knew. In his heart he knew that everything he saw and everything that happened was true. His friend Wise Bird had a twinkle in his eye every time he was with his master. The great raven also knew that all that happened, happened as his master told it.

Epilogue

Om-kas-toe and his people continued their lives of following the buffalo. Only now they had elkdogs. Soon they would have many more of these wonderful animals. Hunting would become much easier and safer. Elkdogs could carry heavy loads. There was more time for everything—art, dancing, music, jewelry making, games, and practicing religion.

The next 150 years or more would be a great time in the life of the Blackfeet people. Elkdogs would be their most prized possessions. They were amazing animals which the Indian people would use to improve their daily lives.

Om was allowed to keep Big Black as his very own. He would ride the beautiful mare proudly. She would produce many colts and fillies in her lifetime. The first of her foals Om gave to Twin Girl. It was a beautiful black and gray colt.

Big Black was a great buffalo elkdog. She could run inches from a wild beast and stay there while Om shot his arrows or threw his spear to down the animal. All the people marveled at the boy, his amazing raven, and the beautiful black mare. They watched him grow into a strong young hunter and warrior.

Om married a fine young woman from another band and brought her to his village to live. Twin Girl also married. She went to live with her husband's people. She lived as her mother had done, a life of love and faithfulness to her family and people.

As Old Man had done many times before, he spoke at a campfire, reminding the people of the birth of the twins. This time he spoke directly to Tall Woman.

"Tall Woman, many winters ago you asked us to let you keep your twin babies. You promised to do your work as before and never to be a burden to your husband or your people. We said the days ahead would give us our wisdom. Woman, your love is great. Your twin children have brought much good to our people. The Above One has given us our wisdom all the days of the lives of Twin Girl and Om-kas-toe. We will remember the power that the love of one woman has shown us from this day and forever."

That was one of the last times Old Man spoke to his people. Soon after he traveled on to the spirit world. Old Man was gone, but his words would never be forgotten by his Blackfeet people.